Still Reaching For The Stars

Still Reaching For The Stars

Published by The Conrad Press Ltd. in the United Kingdom 2024

Tel: +44(0)1227 472 874

www.theconradpress.com
info@theconradpress.com

ISBN 978-1-915494-93-1

Copyright © Paul Allen 2024
All rights reserved.

Typesetting and cover design by Michelle Emerson
www.michelleemerson.co.uk

The Conrad Press logo was designed by Maria Priestley

Printed and bound in Great Britain by Clays Ltd, Elcograf S.p.A.

Still Reaching For The Stars

Paul Allen

Contents

Introduction 1
The singer 1
An American tailor 4
The vagabond 9
The haunted house 15
An accidental murder 19
Rocky 29
The tears of a clown 34
The runner 41
The bank clerk 45
The wrestler 49
One hit too many 52
The opera singer 61
The athlete 66
Death of a shoe salesman 70
Coronavirus 78
On two wheels 82
Mechanically minded 88
The gardener 94

The highflyer	101
To love and to cherish	105
The frustrated housewife	119
The need for speed	124
His father's son	133
Till death us do part	142
No smoke without fire	155
In the name of the law?	166
Call this life?	174
So, you think you want to be a brain surgeon?	185
I have a cunning plan	190
The teacher	205
Silence in court	211
Brush strokes	216
The lasting friendship	226
Santa, where are you?	230
The actor	238
Epilogue: A note from the author Paul Allen	244
Acknowledgements	246

Introduction

Welcome to *Still Reaching For The Stars*, my second book after *A Star In His Own Imagination.* That was a personal memoir, this is a collection of short (sometimes very short) stories, or moral fables, but as my personal circumstances are, to put it mildly, unusual, perhaps I may be forgiven a little personal autobiography before they start.

Over the years, I have had a very active life in many respects, especially on the stage as an amateur actor and singer. I am in a way still in the hope that one day I will be discovered! But admittedly, at my time of life, and given those circumstances, that is not very likely.

Over the years, I have met or worked with quite a few professional actors or singers. One of the music therapists saw a DVD of me singing at a concert with two friends, he said afterwards that I could have been on the West End stage, and I hope he didn't mean sweeping it! One of my friends after reading my previous book said that my life has been like a rollercoaster, I suppose that he was right. It has been full of ultra-highs and ultra-lows.

Five of my happiest times were as follows:

1. When I sang in a choir at the Royal Albert Hall in front of 5,500 people.

2. When I sang with the choir of Kings College at Cambridge Cathedral.

3. When I performed my first professional role of the Pirate King in *The Pirates of Penzance.*

4. Our wedding day when I married Liz on Saturday 20 July 2002. I had proposed to her at the Trevi Fountain in Rome.

5. When Liz and I moved into our big Victorian house.

Five of my lowest moments were:

1. When my brother Dave died

2. When my mum died.

3. When I woke up from my coma in 2012 and realised that I was paralysed and could not speak.

4. When I first realised, I would never see my love Lia again. Lia and I met when I was eighteen and she was twenty-one, she had come to the UK to study English. She was staying with the local vicar so we saw a lot of each other as I spent quite a lot of time at the church, I was in the choir and had a lot of friends there too. We fell in love. The next three years we saw each other as often as we could, either in the UK or in Italy where I stayed with her family. We got engaged but without the Knowledge of her father because we were young and both still studying, me to be a structural

engineer and Lia to become a professor of languages. Lia's father found out and was very angry, he did not want his daughter to marry a penniless Englishman, so forbade us to see each other again. That was the end of my first real love. We did see each other again about three years later when I was doing a holiday tour with my then girlfriend. She was with her boyfriend and we spoke together for a while and then parted with, apparently, no regrets. I still miss her.

5. When our golden retriever Mega died.

At this point, for the benefit of those who have not read my last book, *A Star In His Own Imagination*, I should explain that in 2012 I had a severe stoke which left me paralysed and unable to speak.

After more than six long years at the Raphael Rehabilitation Hospital I am finally living at home and very nice it is too. The staff at Raphael Hospital looked after me very well but as Dorothy said in *The Wizard of Oz* 'there is no place like home.' Now I have ten carers who look after me twenty-four hours a day.

Since my stroke I have learned many things but the most important one is this: it is important to focus on the things you can do now, not on the things you could do in the past.

In my previous book I forgot to mention several

of my friends to whom I can only apologise. One person who I really should mention is Brenda Searle, she played the part of Tzeitel in *Fiddler on the Roof*, when I was playing Motel, the tailor she marries. Brenda has also directed two of the stage shows, have been in, *Iolanthe* and *Rag Time*, she has also played the part of my mother in *Iolanthe* but we will not dwell on that.

My last book alluded to the fact that I have written some short stories and the rest of the book will be devoted to those. Those people who have read my previous book will recognise the first story. Although it is fiction it is based on my life. It is my hope that the second part of my story turns out to be prophetic.

From Liz Allen, Paul's devoted wife

Paul was a very healthy and active fifty-six-year-old man. He had no health problems until one weekend when he developed a blinding headache which lasted until the Monday. On Tuesday he woke up saying his head was still bad but different, and he was numb all down one side. This was a prompt to me to phone for an ambulance.

We did not know that this was the start of a devastating brain stem stroke which would change his life forever.

Paul has been left with Locked in Syndrome which means he is completely paralysed, unable to breathe without a ventilator. He is also partially sighted, deaf in one ear and unable to speak. He is able to communicate by blinking his left eye through the alphabet and building up words letter by letter. This is how he writes his books, by blinking dictation.

Not being able to speak or move is a challenge for Paul as he was a great talker and always used his hands to help the story along. Paul has retained his sense of humour and continues to love telling jokes and long stories to his numerous friends.

This book is a collection of short stories, some from his imagination, others adapted from something that happened in his life. He has had an eventful life so has been able to adapt and enlarge on something that did happen.

Because Paul is totally paralysed, he is unable to do any of the things he did in his life before the stroke. He does spend a lot of time thinking, he has a very good brain and is able to work out a plot from something he remembered from years ago. Or he will plot a story from beginning to end and remember everything he has plotted.

It is such a good thing for him to do as he is using his brain and it takes his mind away from his severe disability for a while.

The singer

Dave had been singing for as long as he could remember. When he was just seven, he joined a church choir to see if he had any future as a singer. The choir master recognised that he had a pleasant voice but in dire need of training.

Dave proved to be a model student and took to the training extremely well. The choirmaster was pleasantly surprised at Dave's progress and, within a year of joining the choir, he was singing most of the solos.

At the age of fifteen, his voice broke, and he spent the next few months anxiously waiting to see if he would be blessed with a reasonable singing voice. While he was waiting, all he could sing was very high and very low, with nothing in the middle. When his voice finally settled down, he seemed to be singing bass but in time it mellowed into a fine baritone.

Dave carried on singing in the Church choir for

several years, until he discovered the world of operatics. He joined his first operatic group at twenty-four and after only two shows singing in the chorus, he started to play main roles.

After playing leading roles with several operatic societies, he was much sought after and landed some parts without auditioning.

After a long and successful career on the stage, he started to perform in some concerts for various charities.

He was also an active person, so it came as a big shock when he had a severe stroke which left him able to do extraordinarily little.

He spent all day either watching TV or listening to music. He would dream of a lot and his dreams were very realistic, as if he had returned to his old life. One dream kept recurring in which he was singing in a concert. In one of his concert dreams, he was singing better than ever. Unfortunately, after a few minutes he woke up to the hard reality that he was paralysed and unable to speak.

Dave loved his dream world in which he could walk and talk normally. He dreamed of holding and kissing his wife, he dreamed of driving his Maserati and riding his Harley Davidson. He also dreamed of playing golf and tennis and going to the pub with his mates. The last thing he dreamed of was eating fine food and drinking fine wine.

Then one day he woke from his dream only to find that he was no longer paralysed. He knew that he had many months of physiotherapy ahead of him before he could walk again but at least it was a start. In the months which followed his feeling was gradually restored to him. Within three months he was off his ventilator and the tracheostomy had been removed. He then started months of speech therapy to teach him to talk again. Once he could talk again, he tried to sing and found that his voice was better than before. He immediately phoned some of his friends to arrange a concert.

When the day of the concert arrived, he approached it with eager anticipation and when it was his turn to sing, he found it so moving that it brought a tear to his eye. He made himself a promise there and then that he would never again take anything in life for granted. Now he had been to hell and back he could appreciate things much more.

An American tailor

Joe Polvicino, a second-generation Italian born in America, had owned a small tailor shop in the Bronx for ten years. Joe was quite the perfectionist, he used only the finest fabrics to make his suits, and he knew that they were superbly made and would sell in up-town New York for three or four times the price, but he had never been bold enough to make the move. Besides he liked his neighbourhood and some of his customers had been loyal for years. He knew that he should increase his prices, but he didn't want to lose his poorest customers.

This may not have been the best area of New York, but all his customers had always been pleasant, and he had always been nice to them, so he had never experienced a problem... until today. He had often dreamt of going to visit his relatives in Italy but, bearing in mind his overheads and the pitiful amount he charged for a suit, this was not likely to happen at any time soon.

One Monday afternoon, two heavily set muscular gangster types strode into the shop. They obviously did not require a new suit, although the state of their attire suggested otherwise. The second man shut the door with the finesse that you might expect from a Neanderthal.

The first man spoke in a heavy Bronx accent, 'How's business doing?' Rather rashly, Joe said that his business was doing well. Quickly latching on to this, the first man said 'you have a nice place here. It would be a shame for any 'catastrophe' to befall it. Joe had never been the victim of a shake down before, but he know that was exactly what this was. He knew also that the hidden message was that if he didn't pay, something would happen to his shop. The first man added, 'we could provide a comprehensive insurance cover which would ensure that nothing ever happened to your premises. This would cost you only 500 bucks a month.'

Joe knew he would never make his fortune from the business, but he was not going to give any of his hard-earned cash to these two creeps. The second man said, 'would you like to pay your first instalment today?'

Making up the first excuse he could think of Joe said 'Monday is not a good day for cash flow. I receive all orders on Monday, but few people collect and part with their cash on Monday.' He asked if he could pay the next morning to give him time to get the money together. Reluctantly the two thugs agreed and departed. As soon as they had gone Joe got on the phone to his brother-in-law who happened to be a detective lieutenant in the local police department.

Early the next morning the lieutenant lay in wait in the shop with four of his detectives. Fortunately, they didn't have long to wait because, at nine o'clock, the two thugs arrived. They strode into the shop and without ceremony demanded their money. As Joe was handing over the 500 dollars the police pounced. They arrested the two thugs for extortion and took them to the police station. In the interrogation room the detectives used considerable coercion and a certain amount of plea bargaining until one of the thugs cracked and revealed the name of their boss. The lieutenant immediately recognised the name as someone suspected of several offences including murder but owing to his mafia connections he had never been convicted. Realising that the case had far wider implications than he first thought, the lieutenant had no choice but to inform the FBI. Within a few hours three special agents from the FBI arrived and instead of assisting, they took over the case.

When Victor, the boss of the two thugs, heard

about the arrest, he felt obliged to contact 'The Family'. He explained the problem briefly and was ordered to come and see them. The thought of meeting the Mafia family was daunting enough but when Victor stood in front of the Don, it was far worse. He explained that two of his assistants had been arrested and now the police were digging for more information. This came as quite a revelation to The Family and left the head of The Family no choice but to sever all links with Victor and the two thugs.

Receiving a phone call from one of their informants, the FBI were made aware that the Mafia were no longer associated with the two thugs or Victor. Reluctantly they decided to withdraw from the case and hand it back over to the police. The lieutenant was delighted to have the case back and soon had Victor arrested and charged. He discovered that there was a court session available in two weeks' time, so he booked it immediately. With advice from his lawyer Victor copped a plea for several offences of which he was suspected. He omitted the murder case because this was by far the most serious offence, and he thought it very unlikely that the police would ever be able to pin it on him. The judge took great delight in passing the most severe sentence the law would allow. Similarly, the two thugs no longer enjoyed the protection of the Mafia, so they were found guilty of extortion and sentenced accordingly.

The powers that be were delighted with this conviction and soon afterwards the lieutenant received a long-awaited promotion. Joe knew nothing of the court case. All he knew was that he was no longer bothered by the thugs.

Joe continued making much appreciated high quality suits for his customers without further intimidation. He never told his wife or family of this episode, and he made his brother-in-law swear to never tell his wife.

The vagabond

Tom lay on the cold hard pavement wondering how things could have possibly come to this. Only a few months ago he had a beautiful wife called Anna and a lovely daughter called Lucy. He also had a spectacular six-bedroom detached house in a very expensive part of London, albeit with an enormous mortgage. He wore suits from Savile Row and drove a Maserati with a very large loan. Now he was sleeping rough and for eating he relied on the coins that were thrown by the passers-by.

It all started about a year ago when he started to drink a bit more due to pressure at work, he also started to gamble, and he fooled himself into thinking that it was only recreational. The final straw came when he began to take drugs, soon his habits became addictions and he started to take a few days off work. He wasn't performing very well when he was at work so eventually, he was sacked. He worked his way through his savings then he stopped paying his bills. Finally, Anna had taken enough so she left him taking Lucy with her.

After three months his electricity supply was cut off along with his phone. He also got a very angry letter from his gas supplier. A month later his house was repossessed and his car. The house was only sold for enough to cover the mortgage. The car sold for enough to pay off the loan with a bit left over. He knew that he would be living on the streets so his clothes would be no use to him. Therefore, he took them all to a charity shop and he bought things more suitable for living on the streets. Now he found himself sleeping on a cold pavement, the only thing protecting him from the pavement was the overcoat which he kept on all the time and a blanket which he slept on. He also had a sleeping bag and a blanket on the top.

He managed to kick his addiction to alcohol because he had no money. Similarly, he could no longer afford to gamble. The drugs were more of a problem. He tried to go cold turkey which gave him terrible shivers, shakes and pains in his stomach. Finally, he recovered after two long months. Now it was only autumn and he wondered how much worse it would have been had it been winter.

In truth he was still very much in love with Anna, but he expected the marriage to end in divorce. Today was like every other day and he spent the whole day begging for money. He hated to do this, but he had to eat. One day, among the other passers-by, he spotted a very well-dressed city gentleman. He recognised the handmade Savile Row suit and handmade shoes. The gentleman also wore a black bowler hat, carried a copy of the financial times and a very nice leather briefcase. He drew a handkerchief out of his pocket and along with it came a lottery ticket The man didn't notice the ticket as it fluttered to the ground, but Tom saw the ticket and quickly retrieved it. When he looked at the ticket, he saw that none of the games had been played. He felt rather guilty, so he tried to call after the gentleman, but he was already out of sight. Tom started to scratch the numbers of the smaller games, but he had won nothing, then he started to play the main game and to his complete surprise he found that he had won the jackpot of one million pounds. He phoned the number given on the ticket and, as he was of no fixed address and no longer had a bank account, he would have to collect a cheque from head office.

He stared at the ticket again in utter disbelief that he had won a million pounds. This money would transform his life into some semblance of his old life. He gathered all the coins that had been thrown to him that day and with it he bought a sandwich leaving enough for the tube fare to the lottery head office. Once he had the cheque, he opened a bank account and deposited it. He then bought a three bedroomed, semi- detached house for £600,000 in a nice part of London. Finally, he bought new clothes to make him look respectable and he bought a mobile phone so he could keep in touch with the estate agents and the solicitor. He also checked int a hotel to await the completion of the sale. He didn't expect the completion to take long because he had paid the deposit in cash, and he would pay the balance in cash.

Finally, he moved into the house, and he filled it with very tasteful furniture, then, assuming that her mobile number had not changed, he phoned Anna. Anna answered the phone within three rings and when she realised that it was Tom, she was both surprised and delighted that he was ringing her. She agreed to meet him for coffee the next day at a place convenient to them both.

The following day Tom arrived at the coffee shop only to find that she was already there. To his surprise she greeted him with a warm embrace and a kiss, she said that it had been a very long time and she had missed him terribly. Then she confessed that she had never stopped loving him. He felt warm tears well up in his eyes and he was determined not to let them fall. Anna had brought

Lucy with her, and she too hugged and kissed her Daddy, and she said 'I love you Daddy'.

Tom found that he could hold back the tears no longer, so he let them roll down both cheeks. Then all three were crying, Tom explained what had happened in the last few months and they listened with interest then he proposed that they both should come to see his new house the following day. They both agreed. The following day Tom awaited them with eager anticipation. When they arrived, he greeted them with a hug and a kiss, and he took both their coats. Then he gave them the guided tour of the house explaining that it was only a three-bedroomed semi-detached house, so it was nowhere near as impressive as the veritable palace that they used to live in. However, at the end of the tour they both agreed that it was cosy and that they loved it. Spurred on by their kind remarks he took the biggest risk of his life and asked them both if they would move in with him, the next weekend. To his great surprise they said yes, they all cried and had a group hug. Then they all sat on the sofa and talked for hours. Tom announced that he had been clean for months and he promised to keep it that way.

Tom went out the following day to buy a bottle of champagne he would keep it in the fridge and open it when they moved in to mark the occasion.

The weekend came very quickly, and they arrived in Anna's car laden with several suitcases which Tom helped to bring into the house. Once they had settled in, he told them that now he had a permanent address and a bank account, he would look for a job. He did not expect to earn the same sort of money that he was once on. He no longer wanted to wear suits from Savile Row or to drive a Maserati, but he would buy all his suits off the peg, and he would buy a Volvo. What mattered is that Tom and Anna loved each other.

The haunted house

As soon as he was old enough to read adult novels, Joe Foxton started to show a predilection for ghost stories. By the time he had been reading for one year this had become an obsession. Now he was twenty-three years old his obsession meant that he only read ghost stories.

One day he was reading his newspaper when he spotted an advert asking for volunteers to spend a whole night in a haunted house. There would be no pay but if anyone lasted for twelve hours, they would win ten thousand pounds. Joe applied immediately but unfortunately so did several hundred others and all applying for only eight places. There then followed a series of gruelling interviews to the eight lucky people. Joe was one of the lucky ones and got through.

Joe was told to meet the others at five to eight on a certain date outside the haunted house. He did as he was told and at exactly eight o'clock one of the organisers arrived and led them into the house. There were five bedrooms upstairs and three reception rooms downstairs so everyone could be allocated a room.

At the start of the night nothing much happened except that they heard the whistling of the wind, the creaking of floorboards and the squeaking of the doors. Everyone dismissed them as sound effects laid on by the organisers but what they heard was real. Then at three minutes past twelve Joe saw his first ghost. The ghost appeared from nowhere, but it was a little old lady sitting in a rocking chair and doing her knitting. Joe was alarmed by its sudden appearance, but it posed no threat to him, so it did not unnerve him in the slightest. Similarly, equally benevolent ghosts appeared to the others. Only two people were unnerved because they did not expect to see a real ghost, although the ghost would do them no harm they packed up and left.

At two o'clock the second ghost appeared. It walked straight through the wall. Joe's ghost proceeded to tear off one of its arms and then began to eat it in front of him, it posed no immediate threat to Joe, revolting as it was, he was determined to stay. The other four people were visited by equally gruesome ghosts, unlike Joe they all lost their nerve and left.

Joe knew that some of them had left but he did not know that he was now all alone. He felt the tension mount inside him as he waited for the next thing to occur. He waited for half hour, but nothing happened. Then at two minutes to three the third ghost made its grand entrance. It came striding through the wall looking decidedly intimidating. It marched boldly to the centre of the room where it began to glare menacingly at Joe. For the first time that night Joe felt uncomfortable. Then the ghost started to run towards him and past right through him. Joe felt an icy chill throughout his body, and he felt violated. Although he had been determined to stay for the duration this was more than he could take so he ran for the door.

Joe turned his head just in time to see the ghost start its second run towards him. He pulled open the door and left the room just in time to avoid the ghost passing through him. Instead, it passed through the wall and stood next to Joe in the hallway. Joe ran down the hall as fast as his legs would carry him with the ghost in hot pursuit. Joe felt very lucky that his room was on the ground floor, and he ran toward the front door. He opened the door and was about to step outside when the door slammed shut. He looked behind him only to see the ghost laughing at him. Joe managed to open the door again and this time he stepped outside before the door slammed shut.

Joe ran all the way home pausing only twice to see if the ghost was behind him, but the ghost had given up the chase. When Joe arrived home, he breathed a deep sigh of relief. The next novel which Joe read was a detective story. He was halfway through a ghost story but it remained unfinished.

An accidental murder

Ken Webster was the manager of a large sales office whose job it was to sell insurance policies to the UK market.

He liked people to call him by his first name because he didn't like to be called Mr. Webster or sir. As he had been heard to say on many occasions 'I have not received a knighthood yet so please don't call me sir.' He managed to achieve and maintain that rare balance of familiarity and respect. The attrition rate in his office was extremely low. Some of the girls of course left to have babies but they always returned. Some left because they were moving to a new house, but no one left for a better job. This was partly because they were well paid but mainly because they were all happy in their job and they knew they would never find another boss like Ken.

Although Ken had a great many staff, he made a point of training them all himself. There were three things that he instilled in them, always be polite to the customer, always treat the customer like a human being and always offer the policy best suited to them without any regard to the commission which they might earn. For this reason, the staff quickly earned the respect of their customers who regularly phoned back for another policy. Ken didn't believe in having favourites but if he did, Gary Taylor would have been Salesperson of the year five years in a row. He was liked by all the staff.

In contrast his life at home was that of a hermit. He lived alone and had few friends if any. He had also fallen out of contact with his family. What Ken and the rest of the staff did not know was Gary had a gambling problem and had accumulated several sizable debts.

Ken was very worried because Gary had not come to work all week and it was already Thursday. This was very unlike Gary who would always phone on the first day if he were sick or needed time off. Ken promised himself that if Gary hadn't phoned by twelve o'clock the next day he would go to his house which was only half a mile away. When the time came Gary still hadn't phoned and as it was lovely weather Ken decided to walk to Gary's house. Ken was only about ten yards form Gary's house when a sense of great foreboding came over him.

When he reached the house, he rang the bell but after two minute no one had answered. This could mean only one of two things. Either Gary was very sick and still confined to bed or he had gone out although the latter seemed very unlikely for Gary. Ken pressed the doorbell again and when he was obviously not going to get a reply, he tried the side gate which to his surprise was unlocked. He opened the gate and cautiously made his way along the side of the house. He knocked on the door not expecting an answer and then to his even greater surprise he found the back door was also unlocked. He opened the door and stepped into the kitchen. He then called for Gary and, although he expected no answer when none came the feeling of trepidation grew. He made his way to the living room and was confronted by a sight which shook him to the core.

Gary was slumped over his desk and on closer inspection, Ken could see the handle of a dagger protruding from his chest. After a few minutes to compose himself, Ken phoned the police, they arrived within half an hour.

The first policemen to arrive on the scene were two young very inexperienced officers who had never dealt with a murder case. When they realised that they were well out of their depth they immediately radioed their sergeant and asked for

CID back up. Now they realised they were dealing with a murder case they took things rather more seriously. Within twenty minutes two senior CID officers arrived. Detective Chief Inspector Simmons and Detective Inspector Lynley. Mr Webster explained to the detectives why he was at the crime scene and how he came upon the body.

The detectives had also brought a scenes of crime officer (SOCO) who busied himself dusting for fingerprints while Mr Webster was being interviewed. The SOCO couldn't believe his luck when he managed to lift a good set of prints from the handle of the dagger, the kitchen table and the back door. However, this is where his luck ran out. When they returned to the station the SOCO ran the prints against the national database returning a negative result. This could only mean one of two things. Either the murderer had never committed a crime before, or he had never been caught.

Two weeks passed with no further progress, so they reluctantly went to Scotland yard for assistance. The following day two burly CID officers arrived from New Scotland Yard. The smug look on their faces suggested that they were thinking 'step aside you provincial types and let the experts take charge.

Another two weeks later they had not unearthed any more clues and evidence leads. Also, they could find no fault in the procedures that the local CID had followed. So, with rounded shoulders crest fallen and somewhat less cocksure than they were when they had arrived, they then sloped back to the yard.

Three days later the local CID got their first break. The publican of a nearby pub phoned the station. He said that a customer had just walked in behaving rather suspiciously. He said it was a local's pub, but a stranger had walked in and ordered a pint. He then sat at an empty table pored over his beer for an hour and a half and left without a word.

He said he apologised if they felt that he was wasting their time, but he had a strange feeling about this. He added 'just in case you are interested I have kept the empty glass behind bar. As Detective Inspector Jeff Lynley replaced the receiver he said to his sergeant, 'this is the third call of its kind that we have had today. News of the murder has obviously leaked and those that know about it are getting jittery. Although this is most unlikely to pan out we have no other leads so we might as well investigate it.' He went to the pub taking Detective Sergeant Ian McTavish and a SOCO with him. Once they had reached the pub the two Detectives interviewed the publican while the SOCO lifted prints from the glass.

Back at the station the SOCO ran the prints against the national data base and not expecting a match he was not disappointed. However, he was both surprised and delighted to find that they did match the prints found at the scene of the crime. An excited Inspector Lynley phoned the publican to ask him to come to the station. Although the publican had a good head for figures, he was useless when it came to remembering facial features. Hence the photo fit that he did with the station artist was at best rudimentary. Despite this it was circulated to all officers.

Three days later two rather portly officers were walking their beat when they saw a stranger a few yards ahead. It was a very small town so between them they could recognise everyone, and they were sure he was a stranger. He also resembled the photofit. The man looked around and when he saw the policemen, he quickened his pace. Although the officers were nearing retirement age and were not as fit as they used to be, they managed to maintain the distance between them.

At this point the man looked around again and when he saw that the officers were still following him, he broke into a run. The officers could not match him, but they did their best. Then the man made a big mistake and turned into a road not knowing that it was a cul de sac. The officers slowed down knowing that their prey would soon be trapped. When the man realised his mistake, he tried one of the side gates. To his surprise it opened so he ran along the side of the house hoping not to find a dog in the back garden. To his relief there was no dog, so he ran the length of the garden and leaped over the fence. The policemen tried to follow him, but they couldn't negotiate the fence. All they could do was watch him sprint across the green towards the flats beyond. The officers may not have caught him, but they had a very good description.

Back at the station the two officers worked closely with the artist to produce a much better photo fit of the suspect. They then turned it into a poster entitled wanted under suspicion of murder. This was widely distributed and within a few days the suspect was apprehended.

The CID had been a bit down on their luck of late, so the Detective Chief Inspector was determined to get a result. When the suspect was caught and brought into the station, the DCI decided to conduct the interview himself and to do everything by the book. Before the interview began Tom Simmons, (the DCI) ensured that the tapes were running, he then introduced all those present at the meeting. This included himself, D I Lynley, the suspect and his council. The DCI cautioned the suspect and asked if he would like to make a statement. The suspect agreed and gave his name as Mark Selby. He quickly confessed to the crime but claimed that it was an accident.

He said that the first time he was contacted by Mr Taylor was about eight months ago, he wanted a substantial loan to settle his gambling debts. One of his creditors was a syndicate who used to hire debt collectors who had no scruples and he wanted to pay this debt before the debt collectors broke both his legs. He wanted to borrow enough to settle all his debts. Having agreed the interest rate and the repayment terms he took out the loan. Six months later however, Mr Selby had not heard anything from Mr Taylor, he had not received any repayments, so he decided to pay Mr Taylor a visit. He said that he only took the dagger to intimidate Mr Taylor; he had never intended to use it. After he had reached the house, he explained how much interest had accrued and demanded that Mr Taylor start repayments with immediate effect. Mr Taylor pleaded for more time to pay. He pointed out that Mr Taylor had already had six months and he wouldn't agree to any more time. Suddenly Mr Taylor went berserk and rushed at him impaling himself on the dagger. He staggered back, turned around and collapsed over his desk.

Neither Tom nor Jeff knew whether to believe

his story but that was for a jury to decide. Soon after the interview had concluded the DCI phoned the local crown court to ascertain the availability of court rooms and dates. He was surprised to learn that owing to a postponement one of the courtrooms was available the following week. He immediately booked the room for the case of the crown versus Mark Selby.

On the day of the trial the two arresting officers and the publican, whose name was Paul Strong, were there as witnesses for the prosecution. Also called were the DCI, DI, SOCO and Ken Webster. Two of colleagues of Gary were called as character witnesses. More of Gary's colleagues were in the public gallery. Mark stood alone. The only person representing him was his counsel. His cousin came but she didn't think that she could say anything that would contribute to the case, so she sat in the public gallery. The charges read out to the accused were as follows, possession of a deadly weapon, manslaughter, murder.

Mark Selby pleaded guilty to all but murder. After the jury had heard all the evidence and the testimonies they retired to deliberate. In less than thirty minutes they reappeared to give the unanimous verdict of guilty of being in possession of a deadly weapon, guilty of manslaughter but not guilty of murder. The judge retired to consider the sentence. When he returned, he delivered the sentence to Mark Selby, and it was considerably less than it would have been if the jury had returned a guilty of murder verdict. It didn't take long before news of the verdict and the sentence had spread throughout the town. There was an outcry that Mark Selby had been found guilty of the back of the police van on the way to the prison Mark had a massive heart attack and died. Except for his cousin no one shed a tear for him. Being a money lender probably did not make him the most popular man in the world, but he did not deserve to die in such an inconspicuous way.

As for Gary, to the police, he was just another case closed. To his fellow salespeople they had lost a colleague and a friend. Although Ken would never admit it, he had lost this favourite salesman and a friend.

Rocky

Rocky was a very large, particularly aggressive, Rottweiler. He lived outside in a dog kennel tethered to the ground by a strong chain which allowed him to roam around the garden but not to leave the grounds. The gateway used to have a wooden gate, but this had long since fallen off its hinges and rotted. A local gang of strays used to taunt Rocky by standing in the gateway and barking, Rocky would run towards them barking and snarling but he could never reach them. What no one knew was that Rocky was so aggressive because he was lonely. He would never allow another dog near enough to become a friend.

Meanwhile a few blocks away there lived Jessica, a diminutive Chihuahua, she was laying on the grass basking in the warm sun, it was the best weather that they had enjoyed in weeks. Suddenly she spotted that the Postman had left the gate open, although she was very happy with her life this was an opportunity to see the world outside and she took it. She was suffering from an infection in both ears which made her totally deaf, so she didn't hear the stray dogs approaching her, she was very surprised when the leader nipped her tail. Jessica quickened her pace, but the strays matched her, and she broke into a run-in order to get away from them, but they still followed her.

Soon she had reached a main crossroad and she saw an opportunity to evade her pursuers. There was a stream of traffic coming towards her and she managed to run across the road before it arrived. Thwarted by the traffic all the stray dogs could do was sit and watch Jessica put more distance between them. The stream of traffic was so long that soon the strays got bored and ran back the way they came.

Two weeks before, Rocky was snoozing in his kennel when the Postman arrived with the daily delivery. He had not yet taken the bundle of letters out of his bag, so he put the bag on the ground and bent over to look for the letters. Rocky opened his eyes to be confronted with the Postman's ample rump, which Rocky found utterly irresistible. He crept up behind the Postman and sank his teeth into his rear.

The scream must have been heard for miles and it brought father to the front door. The Postman explained what had happened then he hobbled away. His parting gambit was, 'that vicious animal should be put down' and 'I'll see you in court!'

Rocky sneaked back to his doghouse. He knew that he had done wrong but also, he felt rather proud of himself. If dogs could snigger, he would have done so. The thought of going to court terrified father so he ran inside to find a defence solicitor for Rocky. He didn't know what the defence would be because Rocky was guilty, and he had acted shamefully.

Two days later Father received the first letter from the solicitor representing the Postman. There then followed a fast exchange of letters between the two solicitors. A week later the Postman returned to the scene of the crime. After the incident he had gone straight to the hospital, and they had given him a tetanus injection and cleaned and dressed the wound. He knocked on the door and when Father opened the door the Postman explained that he had done a lot of thinking and he had decided to settle out of court. Father was delighted and invited the Postman in to discuss the settlement figure. As he left, he added that Rocky would not have to be put down, but Father would have to keep more control over him.

Rocky never knew how near he came to be being put to sleep. Returning to the present-day Jessica looked behind for her pursuers and found that they were nowhere to be seen so she returned to a walk. A while later she spotted a garden with no gate so she thought she would peek inside. She saw a very large sad looking dog and she thought that she would venture inside to have a better look. Jessica only had one paw over the threshold when Rocky started to growl. She took no notice but carried on walking up the path. What a brave little dog thought Rocky. She was not brave at all, she couldn't hear him, so she didn't know what danger she was in. Jessica carried on walking until she and Rocky were touching noses. Rocky rather liked it, 'Is that what it is like to have a friend?' he thought. Rocky appeared to be lonely, so Jessica decided to step into his kennel and snuggle up to him. Rocky didn't seem to mind; in fact he quite liked it.

Meanwhile the gang of strays had changed direction again and were running towards Rocky's house. When they arrived, they were amazed to see Rocky lying in his kennel with the little dog, whom they were chasing earlier, lying next to Rocky. The bravest of the group decided to enter the garden to have a closer look. He walked slowly up the path and stopped after six feet to listen for the bark, but it didn't come. He continued to walk up the path until he had reached the kennel. Rocky looked at him and didn't seem to mind so he dared to go into Rocky's kennel and lay next to him when the other strays saw this, they all walked up the path one by one. Soon they were all lying next to the kennel.

When Jessica woke up, she saw that Rocky was sleeping no doubt having the best dream he had ever had, when she saw this, she knew that her work here was done so she crept out of the kennel and along the path. Then when she left the garden, she trotted home.

Father was pleasantly surprised to see the change in Rocky over the next few days. He didn't know who to thank for this transformation, but he was very grateful.

The strays all became Rocky's friends and visited him every day, so Rocky was no longer lonely.

The tears of a clown

Being a clown was the only career that Sam had ever known. In truth it was the only job he had ever wanted. He had joined the circus in his mid-teens, and he had shown an immediate aptitude for being a clown. Now he had done the job for twenty-three years, he was superb and enjoyed a global reputation for always being able to make people laugh however sad they were feeling when they arrived.

What they could not see was the immense sadness that lay behind his smile. He had felt this way since his wife had died of cancer over a year ago. The same year his brother had died in a car crash. Ten years ago, both of his parents had died of a heart attack and he and his wife had never been blessed with children so now he was all alone. Every night he would return to his lonely flat and cry himself to sleep.

Then one day a beautiful young lady brought

light into his life. Her name was Sophia and she had been to see the circus and had gone backstage to congratulate all the performers. She seemed to spend an inordinate amount of time with Sam. She came to see the circus every day for the next week and always went backstage after the show always gravitating towards Sam. Sam had not asked anyone out since he first met his wife but finally, he plucked up the courage to ask her to go for a drink. He planned to take her out the following night because he finished work after the matinee performance. The time passed very quickly but not fast enough for Sam. He met her at her flat and because he did not own a car, they walked to the pub.

Sam thought that he would be too nervous to talk, and he would not know what to speak about. However, he found her extremely easy to talk to. Also, they seemed to have similar taste in most things including food, sports, politics, music and films. He drank only bottled beer and she preferred cocktails. In no time the evening was over. It may have been only drinks, but Sam thoroughly enjoyed the evening, and it made him feel like a teenager again. Sam walked Sofia home, then he asked if he could see her again. He was overly excited when she said yes, he said he would be free in two days so he asked her if she would be free for dinner.

Sam found himself wishing the time away again but this time he threw himself into his work. It seemed to make the time go quicker and it was certainly better for the audience.

When he met Sophia, they took a short bus journey to the venue, Sophia was very impressed with the venue both outside and in, but she was delighted to discover that Sam had booked them for a dinner-dance. After a sumptuous dinner they joined the dance. The first two dances were fast, and the third dance was very slow. They started to do a waltz then Sophia threw her arms around Sam's neck and for the first time their lips met. Sophia had such a tender kiss that it made Sam feel warm inside and it sent a tingling sensation up his spine.

After what seemed to be no time at all the dance was over and they were back on the bus. Sam knew that the bus went past his flat, so he invited her in for a coffee. His intentions were entirely honourable, he intended to give her a coffee then walk her home. However, one thing led to another, and she ended up staying the night.

The following day, Sam went to his boss with his new-found confidence, and he demanded a pay rise. He explained that while he was living a life of a hermit, he did not need a pay rise but now he was likely to be taking Sophia out quite often he would be needing more money and lots of it. Also, he was one of the main attractions which the circus had to offer. To his utter surprise his boss not only agreed with him, but he also offered him a pay rise. Obviously, his boss was the sort of man who never gave a pay rise to anyone unless it was first requested. Sam was of course very pleased, but it left him wishing that he had been more assertive throughout his career.

He would be working late that night, so he had to wait for the next day to give Sophia the good news. For several months they enjoyed many idyllic dates and finally he decided to ask her to move in. He was worried that it might prove to be too soon for her so when she said that she would love to move in with Sam he was both surprised and delighted, she moved in the next day coming by taxi and bringing with her some of her clothes and few of her possessions. For the next few days, she brought the rest of her clothes and some more possessions. Sophia waited a few months to make sure that this was the right thing to do, then she put her furniture into storage along with the rest of her possessions. She then relinquished her flat. If they were going to move in together Sam's place was the right choice because he owned the flat and it was much bigger than hers.

The next few months were perfect, and he was

ashamed to admit to himself that although he had enjoyed a wonderful marriage, he was happier now than he had been in his entire life. Then he saw Sophia talking to a very handsome young man, they spoke at length then they parted by kissing each other and going their separate ways. Sam wasn't usually the jealous type, but he loved Sophia, and he did not want to lose her. All day he brooded on the subject and by the evening he could not wait to get home and ask her who he was. Sofia confessed that she had been married before, but they had been living apart for the last two years. They were both quite young when they got married and Sophia, after only six months, had realised it had been a terrible mistake. They had both taken their personal things and then they had shared the furniture. All the new furniture which she took was of sentimental value and the old furniture was antique. Sophia had to put everything into storage and then moved in temporarily with her parents while she looked for a flat to rent.

Sophia found an unfurnished flat which seemed ideal. Once she had taken possession of the flat, she took all her things out of the storage. When they sold the house, they had only owned it for a year, so it was not worth much more than what they had paid for it, so by the time they had paid off the mortgage, the solicitor and the estate agent, there was not much left to share. By adding this amount to her savings, she had nearly enough for the deposit for a flat.

Sophia continued by saying that now that she and her husband had lived apart for two years, they were eligible to apply for a divorce by mutual consent on the grounds of an irretrievable break down of the marriage. Sam was shocked at this revelation, but he was also quite relieved. He was only a few years older than Sophia, but he thought that he was about to be replaced by a younger model. Sophia explained that she was meeting her husband to discuss the final details of the divorce.

As expected, the decree nisi came in about two weeks. However, this only confirmed that their application was being processed. The decree absolute would take a lot longer. While they were waiting for the decree absolute to arrive, they went window shopping and Sophia spotted a ring which she absolutely adored. Sam discouraged her by saying that it was much too expensive to even consider buying.

When the divorce was finally granted Sam rushed out and bought the ring. When the time seemed right, he went down on one knee, gave her the ring, and proposed. He was over the moon when without hesitation she said yes and the look in her eyes told him she loved him as much as he loved her.

Within three months they were married, and nine months later baby Michael was born. They both agreed that whatever he decided to be when he grew up, they would support him.

Whenever Sam smiled at the crowd at the circus there was no sadness to hide. He smiled because he was happy. He wondered what he had done to be this happy. They say that what goes around comes around. Sam was only getting back a little of what he had given to thousands of others over the years.

The runner

Will awoke one fine spring morning with the irresistible urge to run. There should have been nothing unusual about his because he was a keen runner all through his teenage years and until he was nineteen. How-ever he was now twenty-two years old, and he hadn't run for two years. For the first year he had too much clutter in his life to even think about running. During the second year he had lost the urge. He leapt out of bed and put on his running kit then he did some stretches and warmups before his run. When he started his run, he kept his pace down and he was determined to run for no more than two miles. By the time he had finished he had thoroughly enjoyed the run and he decided to run every day. Each day he improved his pace and lengthened the run.

One day when Will thought that he was good enough he joined the local harriers. He continued to improve until he was one of the best in the club.

It was suggested that he should do a marathon. He chose to do the less known marathons first, then he applied to run in the London Marathon. Being a member of a running club almost guaranteed that his application would be accepted.

He trained very hard for the London Marathon and when he finally ran in it, he was delighted that his time was three hours and thirty-one minutes. This was extremely fast for an amateur. Of course, everyone was an amateur in the strictest sense of the word because no one was paid to run. However, the elite were given sponsorship so none of them needed any other form of employment. This meant that they could devote all their time to training. Also, anyone who could expect a time of less than three hours was entitled to start the race at the gates. This saved a lot of queuing to get through the gates.

One day Will and his wife decided to go to the West Country for a few days. On the second day Will went for his daily run. His sense of direction must have been off that day because he found himself in the middle of a farm surrounded by farm dogs. They must have taken him for an intruder because all seven of them circled him and started to growl. Will panicked and started to run but one of dog bit him on the back of his leg. The farmer came out to investigate the commotion. He called the dogs off and helped Will into the farmhouse. Two of the dogs were kept as pets, two were strays and only three were working dogs. The farmer looked at Will's leg and then he phoned for an ambulance.

At the hospital Will received a tetanus jab and the nurse cleaned and dressed the wound. He was then told to avoid any strenuous exercise for two weeks. After two weeks of boredom Will continued his training.

Running can be good for you, it strengthens the heart, and it gives you greater lung capacity. It improves your overall health, but it plays havoc with your hip and knee joints. One day Will was training when he collapsed in agony. He went to hospital and after four x rays he was told that he would have to have a replacement for both hips and both knees. This would put him out of action for months, so he would miss the London Marathon.

After the operation, three of the joints were fine but one of his knees developed sepsis. He went back to the hospital where they removed the infected joint. Then he had to wait for a week for the new joint to be made and his knee to be clear of infection. Once the new joint had been fitted, he was fine, but he had to wait for 4 months before he could run.

After the new joint had settled in Will felt as good as new, in fact he was better than new because he was faster. The next time he ran a marathon he did it in just under three hours which meant that he qualified to start in front of the gates in the London Marathon and in any other marathons he could start at the front with the elite.

He entered for another marathon and his new time encouraged him to train even harder. On the day of the marathon, he felt supremely confident. The weather was perfect. It was sunny but not too hot and there was a slight breeze. When he started the run, he was keeping up with the elite in fact he was passing some of them. Finally, he passed one person who was running alone, not realising that he was the leader. When Will arrived at the finishing line he saw that the tape was unbroken, so he assumed that he must be in the lead, sure enough one of the officials came to congratulate him and confirm that his time was two hours and twenty-one minutes. It may not have been as prestigious as the London Marathon and without so much competition, but he had won a marathon.

The bank clerk

Alf had been a bank clerk for twenty years without a promotion. The fact was that he was insufficiently qualified and to be quite honest he was not intelligent enough. He led a quiet almost boring life, and his salary was enough to live on. Then one day he developed a gambling habit. To start with he only gambled online and with exceedingly small amounts, then he found that online gambling did not give him the atmosphere that he craved so he started going to a betting shop. Soon his gambling became an addiction and he started to gamble much larger amounts. He could no longer rely on his salary, so he began to raid his savings. Shortly afterwards he fell into the trap that most gambler's fall into, if he won, he thought that he was on a winning streak. So, he bet again, if he lost, he would bet more so he could recuperate his losses.

Then the day came when he ran out of savings so in desperation, he borrowed £20,000 from a money lender. A month later he was approached at work by two thugs who worked for the money lenders. They demanded some money from him because so far, he had not made any repayments. He explained that he was going through a very unlucky streak and was not able to make any repayments. The two thugs said that he could have another month to pay but there would be two conditions. He would have to pay the full amount which by then would be £30,000 pounds. If he failed to produce the money, they would break both of his legs.

Alf was not sure how he could find such a large amount of money in such a short amount of time. Reluctantly he decided to steal from the bank. Each till contained only five hundred pounds and any over spill was put in a separate box. When the overspill reached £1,000 it was transferred to the vault. Each clerk in turn would spend an hour in the vault to take the money from the other clerks. When it was Alf's turn, he was also asked by the manager to sort out the money into piles of notes of the same denomination. Alf only took two thousand pounds in twenty-pound notes because this would fit easily into his pocket, and he hoped that it would not be missed. That night he took the money home and hid it until he needed it. Fortunately, he lived on his own, so the money was safe.

Every time he was in the vault, he took another £2,000 home, until he had the £30,000 pounds. It was then that the manager discovered the missing money. He interviewed the staff in turn and when it was Alf's turn, he gave himself away by the expression on his face. The manager said that in recognition of the fact that Alf had been with the bank for twenty years he would take the matter no further if Alf returned the money within a week. The only way Alf could see of raising £30,000 was to go to another money lender. With relative ease Alf found a money lender who was prepared to lend him thirty thousand at exorbitant interest. He gave the money to the bank manager with his apologies for temporary loss of sanity and thanked the manager for being so lenient. He then used the stolen money to pay the original money lender.

Months rolled by and he won just enough money to meet the extortionate repayments, but he wondered how he would ever pay the capital sum. Then one day he received a letter from a solicitor asking him to phone the office to hear something to his advantage. When he phoned, he was told that his uncle had died, and he was asked to attend the office to hear the reading of the will. He went to the office and was surprised to find that he was the only one there. It transpired that because he had no siblings or cousins the entire estate was left to him. It further transpired that the uncle was rich.

By the time the house was sold he had enough money to pay the money lender, to pay off his mortgage and to move to a much better area. The surplus money was not enough to live on, but it would supplement his income. He made himself a promise which he was to keep for the rest of his life. He never gambled again.

The wrestler

Ed had been an amateur wrestler all through his teenage years and for the whole of his adult life. Now he was twenty-five and he was exceptionally good. He was already club champion and today he would be competing in the regional final.

It was lucky that Ed did not know that one of the biggest managers on the professional circuit would be watching the match. Ed wrestled well and won with relative ease. In his dressing room afterwards, the manager congratulated him on the fight and then introduced himself. He then offered to take Ed under his wing and make him a professional. Ed accepted, without hesitation and the manager told him to report for training in two weeks.

Ed told his current manager, who said, 'I will be sorry to lose you, but I wish you the best of luck.'

The two weeks seemed to drag, but soon the day arrived when Ed would start his professional career. He reported to his new manager and started his training. Once he had begun to fight as a professional wrestler, he rarely lost a match. After several fights, the day finally came when his manager told him to throw a match. Ed had never been told to throw a match before, but he did as he was told, for fear of losing his job.

After the fight, he regretted losing the match and he decided to do something about it. He wrote to the times, exposing corruption in the game. Soon many others contacted him and congratulated him on his stand. Most of them also said that they too had been the victims of coercion. Spurred on by this reaction he wrote to the times again.

This time, it caused quite a stir, and many more wrestlers wrote to him. Soon it was impossible to arrange a fight. An emergency meeting was convened between six of the wrestlers, representing all the other wrestlers and three of the managers, also representing the other managers. At the meeting it was agreed that all the wrestlers would resume working immediately and in return the managers would abandon the practice of coercing their wrestlers into throwing a match. Of course, there would be complaints from some of the more dishonest managers who stood to lose a lot of money, but frankly they should consider themselves lucky to keep their job.

With renewed enthusiasm the fights were resumed, but before the first match one of the managers took the brave step of taking the microphone from the announcer and addressing the crowd, he said that he had read the article in the times and wanted to reassure everyone that the corruption had been contained and eliminated. Everyone was free to place bets without any fear that the fight had been rigged. Ed continued to wrestle very well almost without losing a match. He never lost hope that one day he would reach the top. He realized of course that he might never reach those dizzy heights but wherever he reached it would be done honestly.

One hit too many

When he was at school Zeke showed no interest at all in any of his subjects, so he did not do any work. He did not even revise for his exams. Consequently, when he left school, he left with no qualifications. The one thing that he was good at was shooting. Sadly, this was regarded as a leisure activity, so it was not assessed. It was a great pity for Zeke that it was not assessed because he would have been top of the class. One exercise which they did was long range target practise. The targets were set at fifty metres and each pupil was equipped with a rifle. Zeke would consistently hit the bull's eye which put him head and shoulders above the rest of the class. Some of his peers could not even hit the target.

Having no qualifications meant that Zeke's choice of jobs was extremely limited. Eventually he went to work for a local supermarket filling up shelves. He tried to kid himself that the job was more interesting than it really was but at the end of the day he had to admit that he was bored. You see he was not stupid he was just lazy, and he saw nothing at school which sparked his interest. Ultimately, he left the supermarket and went to work for his uncle in his shop. Zeke found the work slightly more interesting, but the wages were terrible. Over the next few years Zeke went from one job to another never finding satisfaction.

Then one day he found himself in a pub drinking with a mate. Somehow, they got onto the subject of being a hitman. His friend knew someone who was a hitman and apparently the money was incredibly good. This got Zeke thinking. Here was a chance to put his natural skills to good use but how do you start?

A few weeks later he happened to bump into an old school friend, so they arranged to go for a drink. After they had finished catching up with each other they discussed many things including politics, cars, and football. Then after four pints they started talking about being an assassin.

His friend asked Zeke if he would like to be contacted. With much trepidation Zeke said that he would. Two days later Zeke received the call. The caller obviously knew Zeke's name, but he was careful not to reveal his own name. Also, he did not reveal his address. They arranged to meet the following day in a local park.

The two men sat on a park bench, discussing may things. Then when he had finished chewing the fat, the contact got down to the nitty gritty and he asked Zeke why he wanted to become a hitman. He elaborated by saying that it was not only about being a good marksman, but you had to have nerves of steel and virtually no conscience. Zeke said that because he did have a conscience his weapon of choice would be a rifle. That way he would never have to look into their eyes when he pulls the trigger, and he could think of them as just a target and not a human being, with families and friends who would mourn his passing. The contact said that he completely understood but that Zeke should understand that while he was yet to prove himself, he would only be asked to eliminate low profile victims and his fee would be reduced.

Zeke knew that his priority was to buy a rifle, so after doing his research he decided to buy a Barrett Rifle. This was relatively inexpensive compared to some of them and was more than adequate to do the job. It was however rather noisy, so he also bought a suppressor. Zeke practised with his new rifle to get used to it and to adjust the telescopic sight. He was good at judging distance which was a big advantage in his line of work. He knew that the suppressor would reduce the range slightly, but this would not present a problem because he would never be firing more than fifty metres,

His first three assignments went very smoothly largely because he always did his research and was well prepared. Victims could be on a roof, or in the street, or in a car, whichever was the case he would pick the best vantage point. This could be a window, a roof or even a grassy knoll.

When Zeke was contacted by his handler, he was told that the powers that be were delighted with his performance and the handler had been authorised to give him more high-profile cases with the appropriate increase in his fee. For the next few years Zeke must have taken hundreds of assignments and each time he put the target down with just one bullet. He saved most of his fee and put it in what he called his pension fund. He had worked out a figure which would allow him to retire and live the rest of his life in comfort. Zeke thought that as he had already made a lot of money, he would buy a new rifle but this time it would be a high-powered single shot bolt action snipers' rifle with a powerful telescopic sight. It would take a single fifty calibre high velocity bullet.

For the next few years Zeke showed that he was worthy of his reputation as the only hit man who was a crack shot and always eliminated his target with just one bullet. His rifle was only a single shot, but this had never presented a problem because he had only ever needed one shot. Then one day he was asked to assassinate a Senator. He did not know why someone wanted him killed and he did not want to know. The Senator was going to make a speech on a flat roof of an office block.

Zeke found out that the Senator would have a practise run the day before. He had already decided that he would shoot from the roof opposite, but he used the practise run to pinpoint his exact location. The following day Zeke settled himself well ahead of the Senator arriving. When he did arrive, Zeke got himself ready. As the Senator started to deliver his speech, Zeke got him in his sights, and he put his finger on the trigger. The moment that Zeke fired, the Senator had bent down to pick up his pen which he dropped. Instead of hitting him, the bullet struck the lady standing behind him. She dropped to the floor immediately.

Meanwhile Zeke was loading another bullet, in theory this could be done in three seconds but as Zeke had never practised this exercise, he was not ready to fire again for over four seconds. This was all the time the bodyguards needed to usher the Senator indoors and out of harm's way.

Zeke removed the scope from the rifle and used it to look for the woman who he had accidentally shot. She was still lying on the ground bleeding profusely, but he breathed a sigh of relief when he saw that she was still moving. It was bad enough that he had missed his intended victim but if he had killed an innocent bystander, it would be tragic indeed.

However, on his way home he heard on the car radio that she had subsequently died in the ambulance on the way to the hospital. Later that night the handler phoned him, and Zeke explained what had happened. The handler detected a note of melancholy in Zeke's voice, so he tried to reassure Zeke by saying this is the first time you have missed in almost fifteen years, which is better than anyone else in the history of the company and is something to be celebrated. It is terribly sad that the woman lost her life, but it was no more than a tragic accident.

Zeke appeared to be listening, but he still said that he would be taking the next two weeks off, for a much-needed vacation. But Zeke did not go away, instead he spent the whole time at home brooding over his last failed assignment. He also had time to glance at his savings account and was pleasantly surprised to find that after one more assignment he could retire. He was only thirty-seven, so he was still young enough to start life afresh. If he found the right woman, he would marry and raise a family.

After his two weeks were over Zeke received a phone call from the handler offering him his next assignment but instead of accepting it over the phone, Zeke explained that there were two reasons why he wanted them to meet. Firstly, they had not met for a long time, the only face that Zeke ever saw was the face of his victim just before he killed him. After all, even someone in his line of work needed some personal contact. Secondly, he wanted to say that this would be his last assignment before he retired. Zeke had never seen the handler show emotion before, but he shook Zeke by the hand and said it has been a privilege to meet you, then to Zeke's surprise he gave his name as Ben. Ben then said that the last assignment would give Zeke a chance to right a wrong. The assignment was to assassinate the same Senator who he had failed to kill before. However, this time it would have to be carried out at close proximity. The previous attempt on the Senator's life had made him nervous about appearing outside so all his public appearances would be conducted indoors.

The security would no doubt be stepped up, so Ben handed Zeke a plastic gun which had been commissioned by the company for just such an occasion. The gun would avoid metal detection and the bullet could be hidden in the false heel of the shoe. When Zeke tried to walk through the metal detector the alarm would sound. He would then remove his watch, cufflinks, and any other jewellery. He would put everything in a plastic tray, which he would put on the conveyor belt. He would then attempt to walk through the metal detector again and again the alarm would go off because of the bullet. He would blame the blakey's on his heel's. He would remove his shoes and the alarm would no longer sound.

Zeke said that as the gun would only take a twenty-calibre bullet, he was worried that it would not be powerful enough for the job. Ben reassured him by saying that as Zeke would be working at close range it would be more than adequate. Ben also gave Zeke a special pair of shoes with a bullet already in the heel. He also gave Zeke a set of false identity papers and an invitation under his assumed name.

On the day everything went as planned and as soon as he had retrieved his possessions from the conveyor belt, he made his way to the gents. Once he had entered the gents, he went into one of the cubicles. Once he was out of sight, he assembled the gun and fitted the bullet. He then emerged from the gents ready for action.

At the venue, the Senator started with a meet and greet so he could shake hands with the crowd.

Then he turned and walked towards the podium to give his speech. Zeke saw his opportunity, but he had never shot at a man in the back, and he was not about to start. Instead, he called to the Senator and when he turned around Zeke drew his gun. When he saw the look of terror in the Senator's eyes, he hesitated for just two seconds. This was enough time for one of the bodyguards to draw his weapon and pump two bullets into Zeke. As he fell, his life flashed before him and by the time he hit the ground, Zeke was dead.

They say that he who lives by the sword, dies by the sword. Sadly, that was the case for Zeke. What was even more sad was that there was no one left to grieve for him. Both of Zeke's parents had perished in a car accident the previous year. Also, Zeke had no siblings or friends. One person who would grieve for him was Ben. Zeke died with no will or next of kin so ironically all his ill-gotten gains went to the government who used it for the rehabilitation of juvenile delinquents.

The opera singer

He was born in Tuscany, Italy and was Christened Giovanni Marco Rossi. For the first time aged only seven Giovanni thought that he had a good soprano singing voice, so he joined a church choir. The choir master spotted quite early on that Giovanni showed a lot promise and he started to train his voice.

By the time Giovanni was nine years of age, he was singing most of the solos and the choir started to do recitals at some of the local churches. At fifteen, the inevitable happened and Giovanni's voice broke. With some boys this means that they cannot sing at all for a few months but in Giovanni's case it took a whole year. He spent the time anxiously waiting to see if his voice would return. A year later, he was relieved when he was blessed with a reasonable tenor voice.

Giovanni's voice continued to improve with age and when he was eighteen, he decided to have his voice trained by a singing teacher who specialised in opera. His voice improved exponentially and at twenty-one he applied to the Italian Conservatoire of Music

By this time, he had a fine tenor voice, so when they heard him at the ICM they not only offered him a place but also a scholarship for the first year. This was subsequently extended to the full three years.

When Giovanni first graduated from the ICM he was not fully trusted, so he was only given relatively minor roles. However, he soon climbed up the ranks and by the time he was thirty-seven, he had played most of the leads in operas by Verdi, Puccini, Rossini, Mascagni, Bizet, Dvorak, and Mozart. He avoided operas by Wagner because he had the wrong type of voice. He also performed in some of the best opera houses in the world. Grand Metropolitan in New York, America, Sidney Opera House in Australia, The Royal Opera House in Covent Garden, London, La Scala in Milan and one of the opera houses in Vienna. In short, he had become an international superstar.

Giovanni's career was going extremely well until he was visited by a member of the Mafia. He was told that his voice was excellent, and he was asked if it was insured. Giovanni knew that by insurance the man meant protection. The man said that it would be a great pity if anything were to happen to it but for twenty percent of his income, they would make sure that nothing happened to him.

Giovanni objected to the whole principle of giving money to the Mafia but after negotiations, the figure went down to ten percent of what was a considerable income, he agreed to pay on the proviso that he had nothing further to do with the Mafia. He continued to pay this extortionate amount to the Mafia for years. Then one day the same Mafia man came to say that the fee would be going up to fifteen percent. Giovanni reluctantly agreed to the new fee, but he was already hatching his escape plan. He was not sure how to evade the clutches of the Mafia, whose influence extended to every part of the globe. However, he had a friend who, he was sure, would have contacts, who could arrange a new identity for Giovanni.

Firstly, he was encouraged to take some money out of his bank account leaving the majority in there. Then he was given a new identity complete with a passport and credit cards. He used his new identity to buy a return ticket to Australia. Sadly, someone had to tell his parents that he had perished in a car accident and his body had been burnt beyond all recognition. He hated being part of this deception, but it was necessary for him to disappear. His friend's and his many fans were also told the same story. He was also given a contact in Australia so when he got there, he was given yet another identity. This time he was given a birth certificate in the name of John Travis. He would find the first name easy to remember because it was the English name for Giovanni. He was also given an Australian passport, driver's license, and credit cards. The contact also hacked into various databases to establish his new identity.

John managed to find someone who wanted to go to England but could not afford the fare, so he asked the contact to put the stranger's photo in his passport. John then gave his return ticket and the passport to the stranger. All he would have to do in Italy is to destroy the passport and travel in his own name to England.

John was missing his singing, so he joined an amateur opera group. It was impossible to hide his natural talent so after a short time he was out shining all the others. After about a year he left the society and joined a group of professionals. John quickly worked his way up and soon he was playing all the leading tenor roles.

One day the group was asked to perform at the Sidney opera House. The first performance was exceptionally good, but no one knew that a member of the local Mafia was in the audience. After the show, the Mafia man went to John's dressing room, and he said that John reminded him of Giovanni Rossi. John said, 'a lot of people have confused me with him,' he lied, 'but that is where the similarity ends. I was born John Travis and I have never left Australia, except for holidays. Although I consider myself as a good tenor, I have never thought of myself as an international superstar. Besides, I thought that Giovanni had died.' The Mafia man seemed happy with this because he asked John no more questions. He just wished John good luck for the future and left.

The rest of the performances went extremely well, much to the delight of all the audience and the management had asked them to come back on a regular basis. John had never sought fame and fortune but the thought of singing regularly at the Sidney Opera House made him very happy.

For the next few years, John received several offers from some of the most prestigious opera houses in the world asking him to perform there. To each one, he gave the same reply, 'I am happy to stay in Australia.!' He had established a new life in Australia, and he was content to remain there.

The athlete

Jo had always been a fast runner, in fact, she had been running for as long as she could remember. Her mother would say that she started running as soon as she could walk. All through school, she would win all the running events at sports day, and no one wanted to be her partner in the three-legged race because no one could keep up with her. When she turned fifteen, she joined the local harriers. Although she was the youngest member of the club, she was soon winning all the races.

Then one day, she was approached by a trainer who said that she was already fast, but he could make her even faster. She recognised him as being one of the best trainers in the country, so she said that whilst she would love to have him train her, she didn't think she could afford him. He said that he was already training a few others and he was making a healthy living, so he was willing to take her on for half his normal fee. When she asked him why he would be so generous, he said that she showed a lot of potential. After about a year of working with him she had a good lead over the rest of the runners. He also gave her a sprint finish so she would win each race several metres ahead of the rest.

When Jo was eighteen the club put her name forward to represent Great Britain in the next Olympics. To her delight she was chosen for the squad. When she started training with her fellow lady Olympians, Jo decided to employ the same strategy as she used while she was a harrier. She would start at the back of the pack. Then when she reached the halfway point, she would start to move forward. Of course, now she was running with the elite she did not expect to get very far. She was right because she only made it halfway up the field. Jo was happy with this because she hoped that her sprint finish would get her further towards the front. She seemed to do better when her trainer was there to encourage her. In fact, when he was there, she would come third or fourth but when he was not there, she would only come eighth or nineth. One day when she was training for her favourite distance, the 400 metres, disaster struck. She had made her way to the middle of the pack when she stumbled and took a nasty fall. The runners immediately behind her could not avoid running over her. She was extremely lucky that the girls running immediately behind her had forgotten to bring their spikes or they might have killed her.

After this, Jo tried to get up, but she found that she couldn't move. She had to be carried to an ambulance by stretcher and then taken to hospital. An x-ray showed that Jo had multiple fractures to several of her vertebrae. It was decided to put her into a spinal jacket and let the vertebrae heal themselves.

When Jo returned to the hospital, she had to be admitted because she was paralysed from the waist down. Further x-rays showed that, although three vertebrae had healed nicely, one of them had grown new bone which was pressing on the spinal cord. Several specialists examined her x-rays, and they all agreed that a recovery was totally impossible, and she would never run again. She may not even walk again.

However, she was determined to prove them wrong. After much searching, Jo found a surgeon who was both foremost in his field and was willing to undertake the operation.

The operation was quite major and took several hours, but the surgeon was able to remove all the excess bone successfully.

Jo rested for a few days in bed, during which time the feeling began to come back to her legs.

After she was sufficiently rested, she started her physiotherapy. Jo was unpleasantly surprised to find that her muscles had wasted, due to lack of use. She could not even stand let alone walk.

Through sheer guts and determination, Jo did walk again with the help of two handrails placed on either side of her at waist height. She continued with this technique for several weeks until she was ready to graduate to a walking frame. After a few weeks of the walking frame, she progressed to two walking sticks. When Jo was ready to walk without sticks, she tried to run but unfortunately, she fell flat on her face.

After a few months of learning to walk again, she found that she was also able to run. Of course, she realised that she would never compete in the Olympics, so she re-joined the harriers.

When she could run confidently, she started to run with the rest of the group. She always ran at the back because she had no aspirations to move any further forward. Besides, if she started to feel tired, she could stop and rest without fear of causing disruption to any of the other runners. Jo was just glad to be running again.

Death of a shoe salesman

Al was no ordinary shoe salesman. He was a senior shoe salesman. This meant that if the manager was away, he would substitute for her and run the store. One day he was standing in as manager, with two members of staff. He had just unlocked the door and was waiting for his first customer to arrive. He did not have long to wait before two customers turned up wearing very smart suits. The only strange thing about them was that they both were wearing dark glasses, even indoors. Because they looked very distinguished Al decided to serve them himself. He had a very uninteresting life. In fact, the only exciting thing that ever happened to him was when he sold a pair of shoes for more than one hundred dollars.

It transpired that only one of the men was looking for new shoes. He tried on several pairs before he found a pair which he liked the look of but unfortunately, they were the wrong size, so he was unable to try them on. Al was determined not to lose their sale because they cost one hundred and twenty dollars, so he went to check in the stock room.

As he was returning with the shoes, he overheard the two men discussing their latest hits. Al suddenly realised that they must both be assassins. One of the two men turned around and saw Al listening in the doorway and Al realised that from that moment on his days were numbered. He dropped the shoes and ran towards the exit door at the rear of the stockroom. He then ran and hid behind a dumpster with the two men in hot pursuit. They both started to fire, and Al stood shivering as he heard the bullets ricochet off the side of the dumpster.

When the bullets stopped momentarily, Al assumed that they were reloading, so he made a dash for the main street. Luck was on his side because neither of the two men had a spare clip of bullets. However, they did have spare loose bullets. By the time they had finished loading the bullets into the empty clips and started to give chase, Al had made it to the main street. He managed to elude his pursuers by jumping on a bus just before the driver closed the doors and moved off. Al rode the bus until it reached its terminus which was at the far side of town. After he had disembarked, he headed for the nearest ATM and withdrew as much money as the machine would allow him. He then checked into a hotel and without thinking he used his credit card.

The two men worked for an organisation known only as The Company and by the next morning they had traced Al as having checked into a certain group of hotels. The two men found that there was only one hotel in town belonging to that group, so they headed for it. Al had finished his ablutions for the day and was about to leave the room when he happened to glance out of the window. He saw the two men running towards the hotel and he asked himself, 'How did they find me so fast?' Then he remembered that he had used his credit card to check into the hotel. He was already dressed, and he had nothing to pack so he left the room immediately. He headed for the lift but at the last minute he thought that as his room was on the fourth floor the two men would use the lift to go up, so he used the stairs to go down. When Al reached the last flight of stairs, he waited for the two men to enter the lift. Then he continued down the stairs and walked to the reception. He paid the bill, retrieved his card and left the hotel.

Meanwhile the two men had found his room. They knocked on the door and when there was no answer, they waited a few seconds then knocked again. When there was still no answer, one of them kicked the door open. When they realised that Al was gone, they ran towards the lift but by the time they had reached the ground floor, Al was long gone. Al was heading for the train station and when he got there, he bought a ticket for the train that was leaving first and going to a different state.

When Al arrived at his destination, he looked for a branch of his bank and he withdrew a substantial amount of money from his savings account. Then he went on a spending spree. He bought several items of clothing and a suitcase to put them in. He also bought some toiletries, then he took a short cab ride to a hotel. When he arrived at the hotel, he paid the driver, popped open the trunk, took out his case and checked into the hotel. This time, he remembered to pay by cash. He also decided to use an assumed name. He knew that Jon Doe was not very original, but it was all he could think of at the time.

As soon as he reached his room, he phoned the manager of the shoe store to tell her what was going on and to inform her that it would not be safe for him to return any time soon. For the next few weeks, he moved to a different hotel every two days, sometimes changing towns and occasionally changing states. Living in hotels every day is an expensive business, so after a few weeks he started to run out of money. He knew he would have to draw out some more of his savings account but as he was far from home, he took a risk and used his credit card once only. He wasn't to know that the hotel was not part of a chain but was owned independently. Consequently, when The Company traced him, they were able to ascertain his exact location. When the two men were told, they took a plane to the nearest airport, then they hired a car to drive to the hotel. When they arrived at the hotel, they found that the register had been carelessly left open on the desk. Having obtained a room number for Al they proceeded to his room on the second floor.

Meanwhile, Al was busy packing when there was a knock on the door. He was not expecting room service, so he refused to open the door. The knock came a second time but still he did not answer. After a few seconds, one of the men kicked the door open. There were two men standing in the doorway with one holding a gun. The other man came forward to apprehend him. The gunman had no intention of firing because he had been told by The Company to take Al alive, if possible. However, when Al started to struggle, he was left with no choice. Al could see that the gunman was about to fire, so he ducked. Instead of hitting his intended target the gun man hit the mirror, which was hanging on the wall. As the bullet shattered the mirror, Al thought 'that's seven years bad luck for someone - I hope it's not me!' He was sure that the gun man would fire again so he pulled the other man in front of him. Although the gun man was aiming for Al, he shot and killed his partner. The man slumped to the floor and with Al having nowhere to run the gun man was determined not to miss this time. Keeping his aim steady, he shot and killed Al.

As soon as the receptionist heard the first shot, she dialled 911 and asked for the cops to come immediately. Two motorbike cops were approaching the hotel when the call was sent to all units. They immediately stopped and went to assist. The receptionist briefed them on what had happened, and the cops stood waiting for the suspect to materialise. They did not have long to wait before the man stepped out of the lift. The cops drew their guns and one of them ordered the man to freeze and put his hands behind his head. Rather than complying, the suspect went for his gun. The cop did not want to kill him, so he shot him in the shoulder belonging to his gun arm. Immediately his arm went limp and hung by his side. The other cop approached him, took his gun, cuffed and arrested him. At that moment, a squad car arrived, and two more cops came to assist in the arrest. They put the man in the back of the car and drove to the station. Meanwhile, after the receptionist had given the room number, they went to the second floor to investigate. They found the door wide open and two dead bodies were lying on the floor. They took both wallets for identification and after they had thanked the receptionist for her help, they rode back to the station.

Once they were at the station, they gave the wallets to the sergeant. He searched through each wallet for identification, and he found Al's business cards. After briefing the charging officer, the suspect was charged with double homicide. The sergeant went to his office and phoned the manager of Al's store. He did his best to hide his surprise when he discovered that the manager was in fact a woman, then he broke the tragic news. The manager was devastated by the news of Al's death and for a moment she was silent - then she started to sob. All the sergeant could say was 'I am so sorry.' Al wasn't the best conversationalist, but he was a good man and the best salesman she had ever hired. More importantly, she loved him. It was a secret unrequited love and one she would now have to take to the grave.

Back at the station, the two bike cops were writing their reports. Once they had finished, they gave them to the sergeant to be used for the forthcoming trial. The assassin was confident that The

Company would save him, but they saw him as no more than an insignificant pawn, so they had no intention of interfering. Besides, he didn't know enough about The Company to do them any harm. In short, they were prepared to use him as their sacrificial lamb.

On the day of Al's funeral, the manager locked up the store and all three of them went- she and the remaining two salesmen. Although you can never describe a funeral as happy, it was a lovely service, and the eulogy truly did Al proud. They all gave their condolences to Al's mother before returning to the store.

The manager seemed to be waiting for an eternity for the date of the trial to arrive but when it did, she was in the court room to witness the accused being found guilty on two accounts - murder in the first degree and murder in the third degree. This was of small consolation to her but at least she had the satisfaction of seeing the killer of the man whom she loved brought to justice.

Coronavirus

From an early age Charles seemed to be brighter than the other kids. His mother dismissed this as just wishful thinking. Besides, most mothers thought that their child was better than the rest. However, when Charles started school, he seemed to make little effort, yet he still received glowing reports from all the teachers. He passed the eleven plus with ease and therefore he went to a Grammar school. Again, with very little work he achieved twelve A grade O levels and five A grade A levels. He went on to achieve a first-class honours degree at university. He subsequently joined a prestigious law firm as a Junior Solicitor. He found everything much too easy, and he longed for life to give him a challenge. They say, 'Be careful what you wish for because it could come true.' It was indeed true for Charles because life was about to deal him a challenge greater than anything that he had ever experienced. Charles' career was doing very well until he was struck down with coronavirus.

The word 'Coronavirus' is merely a generic term which is used to describe many different types of viruses, including SARS and MERS. The scientists came up with a word to describe this particular virus which was Covid - 19. Even Covid 19 can affect people in many ways ranging from no symptoms at all to death in the most extreme cases. In Charles case he was quite badly affected, and he had to be admitted to hospital.

He spent a week in a Covid ward after which he took a turn for the worse and had to be transferred to the Covid section of the intensive care unit. Here he spent several weeks and sadly his job was taken over by another Junior Solicitor. However, when he did feel fit for work, he had nowhere to go. He started to apply for jobs and in no time, he had found one.

Sadly, after only two weeks he began to feel unwell again, so he went to see his doctor, who said that what he was suffering from what was called Long Covid. This is where some of the symptoms of Covid return and sometimes hangs around for months. Obviously, Charles lost his new job and when he was ready to apply for another job, he found that it was not so easy. He had been away from the workplace for so long now that he was considered a liability. After several long weeks of waiting a firm decided to take a chance on him and gave him a job

However, the big boss told Charles future manager to only give Charles fairly simple cases to work on to test Charles capabilities. When Charles first looked at the cases, he thought he had joined the wrong firm, because they were easy enough for a child to manage. However, Charles gave them his fullest attention and he finished them in short measure. The manager thought that Charles had put very little effort into these cases and had just dashed them off. When he looked at them, he realised that Charles had put a lot of work into each case. He had summarised each case given a possible way forward and a probable outcome. The manager was so impressed he showed the work to the boss. The boss told the manager to immediately start to give Charles much more complex cases.

When Charles looked at the cases he thought 'this is much better and something I will really have to think about.' Charles was awarded the rank of Senior Solicitor and if the case went to trial, he was able to brief the Barrister and if necessary, he would attend the trial in an advisory capacity. His career went from strength to strength, and he was soon known as the solicitor who never lost a case. With-in two years he was promoted to manager, and it made him think how strange life could be.

He once blamed Covid -19 for destroying his career but now it was at least partly instrumental in giving him the very thing which he had longed for all his life: A Challenge!

On two wheels

Ray had always felt close to his older brother, Bob. This was even though they were years apart. At the tender age of just eight, Ray asked Bob if he would take him for a ride on his motorbike. Bob obliged and although it was only a trip around the block, Ray enjoyed it immensely and he implored his older brother to take him for a longer ride the next day. Ray's school was only a short detour from Bob's normal route to work, so, for the next four years he would take Ray to school on his motorbike.

Ray was immensely proud of being chauffeured to school and it only ended because Bob left the family home and moved to a flat which was much nearer to his place of work. As soon as Ray reached the age of seventeen it was no surprise that he bought a bike instead of a car. In those days you could ride a bike of up to 250cc, but this was not fast enough for Ray. Shortly after he had passed his test, he bought a bike which was much bigger and considerably faster than his 250cc. He started to ride very irresponsibly, always riding well over the speed limit and pulled wheelies in built up areas. Once he even rode past a police garage at twice the legal limit not noticing that there was a policeman in the Rover, so, as soon as he saw Ray, he started to give chase. They could easily match his speed because it was a three-point five litre engine, but they were unable to match his acceleration. The bike was a two-stroke, so under hard acceleration it tended to smoke a lot. This made it impossible for the police to read his registration number.

Ray was oblivious to the fact that the police were following him, but as soon as he realized, he accelerated much harder and lost them easily. When he was sure that they were no longer behind him he turned into a housing estate. He waited there until he was sure that the police had gone before returning to the main road and doubling back the other way. Ray continued with his outrageous riding until he heard that one of his friends had died in a high-speed motorbike accident. This was the third of his friends who had died in bike accidents in a month. It made him think of his own mortality and he slowed down a lot. He also stopped doing wheelies.

One day, on his way home from work, Ray was riding well within the speed limit when a bus suddenly pulled out immediately in front of him. The driver gave no indication and obviously he didn't even glance in his mirrors. Ray had no chance to avoid him, so he slammed into the back of the bus.

Ray woke up in hospital having sustained a concussion, seven cracked ribs, multiple fractures to his collar bone, both arms and one leg. The bus driver had evidently not even noticed the impact because he kept on driving on his merry way. When he returned to the bus garage, he probably inspected the bus and wondered where the dent in the rear had come from. While Ray was recovering, he couldn't help thinking that if he had been riding at his normal speed he would have been long gone before the bus pulled out. What he wasn't thinking was that if he had hit the bus at his normal speed, he probably would have died.

After a few months he was discharged from hospital and ready to ride his bike again. However, his bike was a write off, so after some dispute with the insurance company, they paid up. Ray put some money towards it and bought a Honda Black Bird. This was capable of a top speed of two hundred miles per hour, so Ray rode even faster than before.

His best friend, Pete, suggested that a few of them went on a tour of Europe to blow off some steam.

Five of them took a month off work and embarked on a tour around Europe. Ray and Pete were riding solo, and the other three were riding with their partners as pillion passengers. All the bikes were 1000cc, so they were all capable of cruising at very high speeds.

They planned the journey but halfway through they were itching to ride fast, so they deviated off their route and headed back to Germany. Once on the Autobahn, they started to cruise at some very high speeds. They would take it in turns to lead the pack, to alleviate the boredom.

At one point, when Ray was riding at the back of the group, he suffered a front tyre blow out. He had no time to react because they were doing one hundred and eighty miles per hour. So, Ray was thrown over the crash barrier and into the grassy central reservation. Before he landed on the grass, he head butted a tree at speed.

Meanwhile, Ray's bike was sliding on its side, ruining the fairing and the side of the engine. Then the bike hit the crash barrier, flipping it over, causing damage to the other side.

When the others saw what had happened, they pulled over to the hard shoulder and parked. When it was safe to cross the motorway, they walked back to examine the damage. The bike appeared to be a write off, so they carried on walking towards their friend. The petrol tank must have been leaking because, soon after they had passed, there was a loud explosion. When they turned round, the bike was in flames.

Ray was not moving so they thought he was dead, but when they reached him, they were able to find a pulse, so they knew he was only unconscious.

Ray was obviously in a bad way, but he appeared to be stable, so Pete offered to go and find an emergency telephone. The ambulance coordinator spoke surprisingly good English and when Pete had explained Ray's location, she said that the ambulance would be there in twenty minutes. She also stressed that no one should attempt to remove his helmet.

He then spoke to the breakdown services. Their English was not so good, but between their broken English and Pete's scant knowledge of German, he managed to explain the location of the bike and that they were to pick up burnt remains.

Pete ran back to where Ray was lying to tell his friends not to remove the helmet. Sadly, he was too late. They had already taken his helmet off and with it came the top of his head. Ray had died instantly.

The ambulance arrived in just 19 minutes, and

the paramedics, who also spoke remarkably good English, examined Ray's body and said that the injuries were so extensive that he would probably have died in the ambulance. All they had really done was free him from his pain.

After that, riding fast had lost its appeal for all of them, so, as soon as the bike had been recovered, they rode slowly to the next town. Once they had arrived, they checked into an hotel for the night. When they had unloaded their bags, Pete phoned Ray's parents to break the tragic news. There was silence over dinner, it had not yet sunk in that they had lost their friend.

The following morning, they all decided to cut short their tour, so they headed straight for the ferry. Once they were at the port and had explained the circumstances, it was easy to change their tickets. As the next ferry was not full, they could board.

When they reached England, Pete headed for Ray's parents' house, in order to offer them his condolences, and to tell them where their son was. The others went home, but the following day they all went to Ray's parents' house to also offer their condolences.

Soon after this they all sold their bikes and bought cars instead. It had been fun to ride fast on bikes, but those days were over.

Mechanically minded

At the age of just six, Tom started to take apart anything mechanical. Unfortunately, he was too young to know how to put them back together again, so Dad always came to the rescue, and he helped him. The first thing which Tom took apart was Mum's vacuum cleaner. Mum despaired when she saw Tom sitting in the middle of the lounge floor, surrounded by bits of vacuum cleaner. Dad could hear his wife screaming from his man-cave at the bottom of his garden, so he came running. When he reached the house, he found his wife in hysterics. He managed to pacify her and then he sat next to Tom and calmly showed him how to put it back together.

At the age of ten, Tom's Dad asked Tom if he wanted to watch him working on his car. When Tom reached his teenage years, his Dad allowed him to help. For Tom's sixteenth his Dad bought him his first car. Tom knew that he couldn't put it on the road for another year, but there was plenty to do before the car would be road worthy. This gave Tom the opportunity to practice his new-found skills. His Dad let him lead this time, with him only helping and giving him advice when necessary.

By the time Tom was seventeen, the car was ready for its MOT.

Now the car was ready for the road, Tom's Dad bought road tax for the car and insurance for Tom. He then took Tom out for a drive almost every day for at least an hour. He also paid for Tom to have some more formal driving lessons. So, well ahead of Tom's eighteenth birthday, he passed his test. By the time Tom had to start university, he was able to drive himself there. Tom had been accepted to do a degree in mechanical engineering, but he also took a course in business studies, because one day he intended to own his own garage.

Tom got his degree and went to work in a large garage as a mechanic. This may seem a strange choice for a graduate, but Tom needed the money, and it gave him the experience he would need in later life.

When Tom had gained enough experience, he took out a loan from the bank and bought a dilapidated garage. His Dad then helped him to renovate it and create two mechanics workstations, each equipped with a hydraulic lift capable of lifting a car to head height and a full set of tools and test equipment. Tom's Dad then came to work with Tom as the second mechanic.

Trade was slow at first, but the word soon got around and in just over a month they had more work than they could handle.

Several years passed and Tom found himself in a financial position to pay back the loan in full, but instead of doing so, he extended it and bought a bigger garage. This time the garage needed no work doing to it and was already equipped with four mechanics workstations.

After the move, Tom and his Dad continued to work as mechanics and Tom hired two more. He also carried on with his advertising campaign, this time saying that he had relocated the garage.

Tom's Dad had suffered from arthritis for many years, but just a bit more than a year after the move, it got so bad that he felt unable to continue as a mechanic. Tom gave his Dad the job as supervisor and Tom moved into the inner office to become the manager and concentrate on the running of the business. He then hired two replacement mechanics.

Tom decided that the way forward was to offer to do servicing and minor repairs to prestigious cars, such as Aston Martins, Jaguars, Land Rovers and Bentleys. He decided to avoid Rolls Royce and some models of Daimlers and Bentleys because they were too long for his lifts. He sent the mechanics on courses to learn the specifics of each car and he also encouraged them to use the internet.

Tom made sure that his mechanics were well paid, but in return he expected a lot from them and if any of them were below his required standards, he was quick to replace them. He asked the mechanics to keep their workstations clean and tidy. This was better for them and was better for the customers. He also hired a cleaner for the rest of the garage. If the customers car had an oil leak, he told the mechanics to repair it without delay. This helped to keep the workstations clean, and it delighted the customers.

Tom also decided to start selling secondhand prestige cars, so he had a large extension built to act as a show room. He thought that by keeping to the older cars he could compete with the main dealerships.

Several years later, his Dad had a massive heart attack and died. Tom could not understand it because there was no history of heart conditions in his Dads family. He was fairly slim and relatively fit. He had never smoked, and he only drank in moderation. Whatever the reason was for his Dad's heart attack, Tom was absolutely devastated. He had become even closer to his Dad since his Mum had died.

Tom had no siblings so, as sole executor he had to complete his duties before he could grieve. Everyone has different ways to show their grief, Tom's way was to shut down completely, and for over a month, he seemed to give up on life. He neglected his wife and his business. Bills remained unpaid and he soon received angry letters from his creditors. He did not reply to any of his correspondence and stopped his advertising campaign. Consequently, his trade soon dropped off.

Mainly it was only his regular customers who came, so his mechanics got bored and two of them left.

Before he lost his business altogether, his wife intervened. She said that it was quite natural for him to need to grieve for his Dad, particularly as they were so close. However, the time for grieving was over and it was time to take back control of his company.

Tom knew that she was right and, besides, his Dad would not want him to lose his business. His wife paid all the bills and sent letters apologizing for the delay and explaining the circumstances. She then helped Tom to catch up with his correspondence.

In memory of his Dad, he renamed the garage Charles' Autos, and he informed all his regulars of the name change. He then restarted his advertising campaign and hired two replacement mechanics.

In due course the business was thriving, and Tom was able to hire a new supervisor, a secretary and a sales manager.

Tom inherited his Dads house, and as it had no sentimental value for him, he sold it and bought another garage. After all, his Dad spent more time at the garage than he did at home, and it was not a house he had ever lived I, as his Dad had moved soon after his Mum died.

Tom hired staff to fully equip the new garage. He then hired a new manager for the first garage whilst he stepped back to perform a more passive role. A few years later, Tom was the proud owner of four garages, all called Charles Autos, and he had all of them specializing in different types of cars. The first garage specialized in English cars and the other three specialized in Japanese cars, German cars and Italian cars.

Tom hoped that his Dad was looking down and was very proud of him. Tom knew that he could not have achieved any of this without the help from his Dad.

The gardener

Jack first started to show an interest in gardening at the age of fifteen. This became an obsession, this was unusual for him, he had never been obsessive about anything. His friends spent all their spare time either chasing girls or going to the pub or disco's. On the other hand, Jack could always be found in the garden or glued to the television watching either gardening programmes or gardening DVD's.

Jack worked with his dad for many years, during which time he learnt a great deal. Then his dad was struck with a rare degenerative spinal disease. This made it difficult for him to do manual work. Shortly afterwards his dad's condition deteriorated so much that he had to give up gardening, and take medical retirement, so Jack took over.

At the age of twenty-five, Jack got married and his wife, Sofie agreed to move into Jack's father's house and help with his father's care. By this time, his father was in a wheelchair. The following year, Sophie, in what can only be regarded as a completely selfless act left her job and became the full-time carer. Jack was painfully aware that he was now the only breadwinner in the house, so he took on more shifts at work. Now he had a lot less time to spend on the garden, he had to redouble his efforts. With time he grew in both confidence and competence, and he started to have new innovative ideas for the garden. One such idea was to build a multi-tiered fishpond. Water was pumped from the lowest tier to the top via a filter. Then he cast a big flying fish around the end of the pipe, so water appeared to be coming from the fish's mouth. The water gushed into the top tier then down until it returned to the bottom tier where he kept twelve goldfish. The filter kept the pond crystal clear.

Jack also built a vegetable patch and one day he was digging it over when his wife called out to him asking if he was ready for a break and to have a cup of tea with her. Jack turned his head to accept and, in a moment, of distraction he drove the fork through his foot. When the fork pierced his foot, it was agony but when he took the fork out the pain was so great that he nearly fainted. So Sofie rushed to his aid and when he was able to stand on one leg, she took off his boot and sock to assess the extent of his injury. Once she could see his foot it became obvious that two prongs had gone through his foot, both wounds were bleeding, but one was gushing blood. Sophie applied pressure to both wounds and although she managed to stop the bleeding from one wound, she only managed to reduce the flow of blood from the other wound. She had never received any formal training as a nurse but seemed that she had a certain aptitude for nursing. She helped him to her car and rushed him to hospital. All the way he kept pressure on the wound that was still bleeding.

When they reached the hospital, Sophie helped Jack to A and E. The triage nurse looked at his foot and as soon as she had seen it, she promoted him to the front of the queue. Another nurse cleaned his wounds and by the time she had finished the doctor arrived. He looked at Jack's foot and asked the nurse to administer a tetanus injection along with a strong painkiller. He also asked her to arrange an MRI Scan to schedule an operation for the next morning and to find a bed for Jack.

The next morning the nurse prepared Jack for the operation and wheeled him to the operating theatre. He was given a local antiseptic and he was invited to watch the operation. He declined because he was rather squeamish. The surgeon made two incisions at the site of the two wounds. He then stitched the artery and the two muscles that were punctured using dissolvable sutures. He decided to let the nerves repair themselves. After Jack was stitched up, the operation was declared a complete success. When the nurse had finished giving Jack the injections, she took him for his MRI Scan, which revealed that by some miracle he had not broken any bones, but he had punctured an artery and two muscles. He had also damaged a few nerves.

Later that day Jack was discharged and Sofie drove him home. He was told to rest for at least a month, but it took six weeks before he could stand on it. As soon as he was able to walk, he was back out in his garden. The garden looked sadly neglected having not been touched for six weeks but after Jack had done a bit of weeding and mowed the lawn it was back to its former glory.

After a few years, Jack was reading the newspaper when he noticed an advert for the annual village garden competition. His garden was looking particularly splendid, so he decided to enter. The judges all agreed that Jack's garden was superb, and they unanimously awarded him first prize. It also entitled him to enter the county wide competition.

Until a few weeks before the judging was due to commence his garden was looking at its best. Then one night, he was visited by vandals. When he arose and saw the once beautiful garden he fell to his knees and wept. The lawn was dug up, the flowers all had their heads cut off and they had even punctured the pond, so all the water had leaked out and the fish lay dead on the bottom.

He was sure that this was the work of a jealous rival, but he did not know who. Even if he had known who was responsible, he would have no proof. He was left with no choice but to withdraw his entry. It took a few months to repair the damage but with a lot of hard work, perseverance, and determination, he managed it. He repaired the holes in the pond, refilled it with water and restocked it with fish.

The following year, he entered the county contest but this time he asked the organiser to be very discreet about his entry. Honouring his wish, the organiser kept Jack's entry a complete secret. Consequently, he received no further visits during the night. Everything was going well, until about two weeks before the judges were due. Then came three days and three nights of torrential rain. The rain was so hard that it hurt to go out in it. After three days the flowers were ruined, and the rest of the garden was waterlogged. Again, he had to withdraw his entry and he was told that because the severe rain had not affected the rest of the country the contest would go ahead.

The next year, Jack was plagued with the opposite problem. Only two months before the judging was due to commence there was a record heat wave. This was accompanied by a drought which lasted for six weeks. For the first two weeks Jack used a sprinkler on the grass and he used a hose to water the rest of the garden twice a day. However, after two weeks the council announced a hose pipe ban. Jack struggled on, with a watering can, but eventually the weather won. The flowers withered and the grass turned brown. Jack had to withdraw his entry. However, this time the organiser said that the whole county had been badly affected so the contest would be cancelled. The following year, Jack prayed that the weather might be a bit more kind. His prayers must have been answered because all year the weather was mild and if it rained it was noticeably light. Jack used a hose to supplement the rain and the garden was looking superb. Two days before the judges were due, he gave the lawn a final cut and he weeded the rest of the garden.

The flowers were equally spaced out and grew in a straight line. The day before the judges were due, he trimmed the edges of the lawn with a pair of scissors. His father gave the garden one last inspection and afterwards he said Well-done son, I am proud of you. Even when I was at my best, I never could have produced a garden as wonderful as this'. Jack was overwhelmed. He had always been close to his dad, but he had never received compliments like this. He felt warm tears welling up in his eyes, but he did not dare let them fall because his dad had always told him that real men don't cry. Finally, he could resist no longer, and he hugged his dad. Both men let tears, that had been supressed for decades, roll down their cheeks. Jack had never been so happy.

The next day the judges came and were very impressed with his garden and although they would not say, they all saw him as a strong contender, A few days later, Jack heard that he had won the contest, so he was now gardener of the year.

Together with the time he was complemented by his father, he had never been so happy. Although Jack always kept his garden looking pristine, he never saw a reason to enter a contest again.

The highflyer

For many years Rob's parents formed a fantastic double act on the trapeze. She was a very graceful acrobat, and he was a very good and reliable catcher. Eventually the years caught up with him and this, together with the onset of Parkinson's, meant that he no longer considered himself a reliable catcher, he decided to train Rob to be a catcher.

Initially Rob had reservations about climbing up on to the trapeze but once he was there, he felt at home. For the next six months he rehearsed with his mother, she gave simple catches to start with then they progressed to the more advanced somersaults. Finally, they were ready to perform in front of an audience. They performed very well, and Rob proved to be a very good catcher, but his mother always wanted to do something better. She decided to perform the triple somersault with no safety net. Everyone including Rob and his father tried to persuade her not to do it, but she was determined to press ahead. When the time came, she must have been suffering from nerves for the first time in her life. She performed a very good triple somersault, but her timing was a bit off. Rob managed to catch her, but his grip was at best tenuous.

Rob watched in disbelief and utter horror as his mother slipped from his grasp and fell to her death. The stage crew were very quick to close the curtains, so the audience did not have to stare at the dead body. Meanwhile Rob just stared at his mother's twisted body hoping that it was a terrible nightmare. As soon as the crew had finished erecting the safety net, he dismounted and when he was back on terra firma he ran to his mother. He arranged her body in an attempt to make her look more elegant, then he cried. He sobbed uncontrollably all the while blaming himself for her death. He knew of course that he was not entirely to blame but she had paid the ultimate price so he would not bring himself to blame her for anything. His father blamed him completely for the accident and vowed he would never speak to Rob again.

Although Rob had lost his taste for the trapeze, he still loved the circus, so he sat in the front row and watched every night. Ironically, the high-flying act was replaced by a juggler, a sword swallower, and a fire eater, but after a few weeks the new trapeze artist arrived. She was lovely, petite and with a very nice figure. Rob was instantly attracted to her. She came with her own catcher, but he could only stay for a month because he was on loan from another circus. Rob hated to admit but, in the air, she was even more graceful than his mother. When Suzy came down from the trapeze Rob introduced himself and the two of them found it surprisingly easy to talk to each other. After a lot of persuading, she managed to coax him into going back onto the trapeze. For the next month she trained him as her catcher he agreed with everything that she had asked of him but the only thing that he was adamant about was that she should never perform without a safety net. By the time her official catcher had to leave Rob was ready for the public. He could still see the look of terror on his mother's face, and he never wanted to see that again.

Rob and Suzy performed extremely well together; she had the confidence that however complicated her acrobatics got Rob was always there to catch her. He did not believe in having romantic entanglement with someone who he worked with but inevitably they became an item. His father finally forgave Rob and he approved of the match. Eventually he gave his blessing for firm, so he earned a lot of money. This supported his Casanova lifestyle. He lived in a penthouse apartment, and he drove an Aston Martin. He was extremely popular with the ladies, and he never went anywhere without a very attractive lady on his arm. When he met Maria, he only had eyes for her.

On the first date, he walked to meet Maria at her flat as he intended to take her to a local wine bar. After the first drink, Adam found that he could relax much more. Conversation then flowed freely and in no time, it was time for the wine bar to close.

Adam walked Maria home and kissed her on the cheek to bid her goodnight. He then waited outside her door while she went inside the flat. 'What a perfect, gentlemen' thought Maria. She was attracted to him physically but that was all. Adam had about a mile to walk home, but it didn't feel like it because he was walking on air. They had only been for a drink, but he felt positively euphoric.

For the next date, again he walked her to a local restaurant. They had a wonderful time and when he had walked her home, he chanced to give her a swift kiss on the lips. It was only a fleeting kiss, but it was warm, tender and sweet so it left a feeling stirring inside of her.

and a fire eater, but after a few weeks the new trapeze artist arrived. She was lovely, petite and with a very nice figure. Rob was instantly attracted to her. She came with her own catcher, but he could only stay for a month because he was on loan from another circus. Rob hated to admit but, in the air, she was even more graceful than his mother. When Suzy came down from the trapeze Rob introduced himself and the two of them found it surprisingly easy to talk to each other. After a lot of persuading, she managed to coax him into going back onto the trapeze. For the next month she trained him as her catcher he agreed with everything that she had asked of him but the only thing that he was adamant about was that she should never perform without a safety net. By the time her official catcher had to leave Rob was ready for the public. He could still see the look of terror on his mother's face, and he never wanted to see that again.

Rob and Suzy performed extremely well together; she had the confidence that however complicated her acrobatics got Rob was always there to catch her. He did not believe in having romantic entanglement with someone who he worked with but inevitably they became an item. His father finally forgave Rob and he approved of the match. Eventually he gave his blessing for them to marry. Rob and Suzy continued to thrill the crowd with their act. Suzy's most impressive stunt was a triple somersault with a double twist. It was comforting to have a safety net but because her timing was always so perfect, they never needed it.

To love and to cherish

Maria was an extremely attractive lady of twenty-three, although she only thought of herself as looking OK, owing to her complete lack of self-esteem. Similarly, she only considered herself to be an average dental nurse, but her dentist thought that she was excellent. However, she would soon meet someone who would change her life completely.

In contrast, Adam was a self-assured, handsome young man of twenty-five, whose good looks were only matched by his charm and easy wit. When he first saw Maria, his silver tongue abandoned him, and he was left totally tongue tied.

Adam decided that it was time to see a dentist and when he saw Maria he was besotted. He wanted to ask her out, but he could not find the words. Fortunately, the dentist wanted to see him again and on the second visit he asked Maria to go for a drink.

Adam was a junior partner in a very large law

firm, so he earned a lot of money. This supported his Casanova lifestyle. He lived in a penthouse apartment, and he drove an Aston Martin. He was extremely popular with the ladies, and he never went anywhere without a very attractive lady on his arm. When he met Maria, he only had eyes for her.

On the first date, he walked to meet Maria at her flat as he intended to take her to a local wine bar. After the first drink, Adam found that he could relax much more. Conversation then flowed freely and in no time, it was time for the wine bar to close.

Adam walked Maria home and kissed her on the cheek to bid her goodnight. He then waited outside her door while she went inside the flat. 'What a perfect, gentlemen' thought Maria. She was attracted to him physically but that was all. Adam had about a mile to walk home, but it didn't feel like it because he was walking on air. They had only been for a drink, but he felt positively euphoric.

For the next date, again he walked her to a local restaurant. They had a wonderful time and when he had walked her home, he chanced to give her a swift kiss on the lips. It was only a fleeting kiss, but it was warm, tender and sweet so it left a feeling stirring inside of her.

For the third date, Adam wanted to take her to his favourite restaurant. This was a bit further away, so he picked her up in his Aston Martin. It was a soft top and as it was a warm summers evening, he put the top down. After a lovely meal, he took her home and this time he gave her a long, lingering kiss on the mouth.

Adam was getting bolder by the fourth date, so after giving her a kiss, he also gave her a warm, passionate hug. This time she invited him in to her flat for a coffee.

They talked into the small hours, while drinking coffee and brandy. Then she invited him to sleep on the sofa while she went to bed.

They carried on for the next few weeks, with Adam always sleeping on the sofa. Then one night she invited him into her bed.

They held each other for a long time and before they made love, she confessed it was her first time. She had been saving herself for someone who she truly, loved and she was glad that she had because it was wonderful.

The following day was a Saturday and Adam said that he had to return to his apartment for a change of clothes. However, he went straight into town for an engagement ring. He knew it was a bit soon, but he was sure it was the right thing to do. He returned to her flat with a change of clothes, the ring and a bottle of champagne, just in case they had something to celebrate. Later that night, he proposed and to his amazement she said yes. He ordered Chinese, which they enjoyed with the champagne.

They spent the next few days compiling a guest list. They both have large families and a wide circle of friends, so when the list reached 500, they realised that a church would not be big enough so they would need a Cathedral. Maria didn't think that it would be possible to be married in a cathedral, but Adam assured her that because he had some friends in very high places all things would be made possible. They both agreed that, since the engagement was rather sudden, the wedding shouldn't be for at least a year. This would give them both the chance to reflect on their feelings and decide whether they really wanted to go ahead with the wedding, also, it would give them time to organise the many things which a wedding the size of theirs, world require. The hardest thing would be to find a venue for the reception which could seat 500 people in one room.

Back at work one Monday morning, all the senior partners came into the general office in order to make an important announcement. They said that they had just secured a contract with a big firm. The contract would give them all the firms legal work for a year. If the firm were happy with their performance during the first year, the contract would be extended until further notice.

The partners said that they would hold a big party to celebrate. The party would be held on Friday night, and everyone would be invited, along with their partners. A few of the staff were asked to organise the party. They were given a generous budget to buy a large amount of drink and to hire both a caterer and a DJ. They would also be responsible for decorating the general office.

During the months between Adam proposing to Maria and the big announcement, Adam was propositioned by some of the girls, but each time he declined politely but firmly. They decided to declare him no longer available. They realised that Adam must love Maria very much to have changed so radically. Unfortunately, nobody thought to tell Suzi, the new girl.

The party was a resounding success, and a good time was enjoyed by all. Some of them enjoyed it more than others. A few of the staff, including Adam, drank much too much. Two of the girls were sick and Adam reverted to his old self. Suzi started to flirt with Adam, and because he had drunk too much to know any better, he started to respond to her advances. At an appropriate moment, he dragged Suzie off to an empty office belonging to the director who couldn't come to the party. Similarly, Maria couldn't come because she had a prior engagement.

Suzi and Adam both ripped off their clothes, but before anything could happen, Adam passed out. When he recovered consciousness, Suzi told him that something had happened, and she said that it was wonderful.

They re-joined the party separately so as not to attract attention. They had just returned to the fray when their colleagues started to phone for taxis to get them home. The caterer and her staff were long gone, and the DJ was just packing up his things. Those who had the longest to wait for their taxi started to clear up the aftermath of the party.

The next morning, Adam woke up next to Maria, with an enormous hangover and with no recollection of what had happened at the party. He went back to sleep and when he awoke, his memory was starting to return. He remembered that he had dragged Suzi off to a room, but he could not remember what happened next. Suzi told the girls in the office her version of what had happened between her and Adam. Of course, this was a complete fabrication, but the girls were not to know, so it became the subject of hot gossip for the next few weeks.

During the coming months, Maria and Adam spent all their spare time searching for the ideal house which they could call home. Finally, they found what they were looking for and they agreed to buy it. Adam's apartment was lovely, but it was a typical bachelor pad. Maria gave it the feminine touch, but it would always be his place not theirs.

Adam's apartment sold very quickly because it was a desirable place in a very sought-after area.

After a few months, the long-awaited wedding of Adam and Maria was very grand indeed. The couple were blessed with glorious weather, so Adam's best man put down the roof of his Mercedes sports car before driving Adam to the cathedral Adam had secured for the wedding. A while later Maria made her stately arrival with her father in a horse-drawn, open-top Landau, closely followed by a stretch limousine carrying the maid of honour and several little bridesmaids. The two vehicles waited until the end of the service so they could convey the happy couple and the bridesmaids to the reception. Adam sat nervously at the front of the cathedral, while Maria was having her photograph taken.

The service was splendid indeed. The Bishop of the Diocese was presiding, and they had a full choir, a quartet of professional opera singers, the cathedral organ and a small orchestra. The organist played to announce the majestic entrance of the bride, then he continued to play while Maria glided up the aisle with her father next to her and a long line of bridesmaids behind. Adam resisted the urge to look behind, but when Maria reached his side and he saw her for the first time that day, she quite took his breath away. She always looked beautiful but wearing her designer-made wedding dress and her newly styled hair, she looked absolutely stunning. The organist accompanied the choir, as they led the hymns. When the Bishop had pronounced them as man and wife, Adam and Maria took their first communion together, after which they signed the register in the chancel, where everyone would see them.

During the signing, the opera singers performed three pieces accompanied by the orchestra. After the service had ended, the organist and the orchestra played as the happy couple processed down the aisle towards the doors.

When all the guests had arrived at the rather impressive reception hall. They were all seated for what can only be described as a veritable banquet, compromising several courses. An army of waiters and wine waiters served each course, together with its own wine, chosen to compliment the food.

A chamber orchestra played during the meal. There then followed a period of silence for the speeches. Each speech was very well received, especially the one from the best man. He managed to maintain a perfect balance between telling jokes at the expense of the groom and paying compliments to the newlyweds.

After the speeches, a Ceilidh band played for the rest of the day, finishing at midnight. Also, those who had not already booked their taxi's, were given a chance to do so. Most people had planned to stay in a hotel, but some went straight home. The couple booked a room for themselves and for their best friends.

The next morning, the couple had planned to have breakfast with their friends, but some of them were still nursing headaches from the night before. Some of them still felt too drunk to drive, so they stayed for another night.

Adam and Maria had booked three weeks off for their honeymoon, but they were only going away for two weeks and would not be flying until the Wednesday, so they still had plenty of time to stay one more night.

Everyone appeared to enjoy the wedding, so the couples dearest wish was that the day would be remembered for a very long time.

After a lovely honeymoon Adam and Maria returned to finish opening their many cards and a host of presents. They had four days before they would be returning to work, so they also wrote their many thankyou cards.

Adam knew how much Maria's job meant to her, so he said that if she wished to carry on working for the dentist she should do so. Anyway, it would help to keep her somewhat financially independent. Meanwhile, it left him free to continue using his sizeable salary to pay the bills. This would leave plenty to keep them in the manner to which they were both accustomed.

About two months after the wedding, one of the senior partners in Adam's firm announced that he was about to retire and to mark the occasion, he had taken the liberty of hiring a complete restaurant. Everyone in the company would be invited, together with their partners, but he would also be inviting the CEOs of their most important clients. Adam was then spoken to privately and offered the chance to become the next senior partner. The only condition was that he could raise enough money to buy the retiring senior partners shares in the company. They gave him an approximate value and Adam was confident he could raise the money by selling a few of his investments. He accepted the kind offer, knowing what the position would entail.

The meal was a civilised affair compared to the office party. The host made it very clear that everyone should order what they wanted, both in terms of food and drink. He would then foot the whole bill.

After a few drinks, people's tongues became a bit looser and the girl sitting opposite Maria let slip a few details of Adam's indiscretion with Suzie. This was the first time Maria had ever heard about it, so she was both furious and embarrassed in equal measure. However, she knew that this was neither the time nor the place to vent her anger, so she decided to wait until they got home.

When she got him home, she exploded with rage, she was partly Spanish with a typical fiery Latin temperament. Therefore, Adam was amazed that this was their first row. She said 'I can live with you always working very long hours, so we barely eat together. I can just about cope with the fact that you seem to pay more attention to your work than to me. However, the one thing that I can never accept is you being unfaithful to me'. She then told him to sleep in one of the spare bedrooms.

In the morning, Adam hoped that Maria might have calmed down, but she was just as angry, and she told him to pack his bags and go. Adam wanted to argue but he knew he was guilty, so he left and checked into a local hotel.

Every day Adam wanted to phone Maria, but he knew that she needed space.

A few days later, Adam did phone her and asked if she would meet him at a local wine bar. When she arrived, Adam said that they needed to discuss the future but all she could talk about was divorce. Adam was shocked, and he pleaded with her to come with him to a marriage guidance counsellor before she went any further.

At the first session, Maria said that Adam's infidelity had made her incredibly angry. Adam said that he was deeply sorry, but he would never have done it, he had much too much to drink.

Maria thought that they would only have one session, but they ended up having four. At the last session, Maria said that she still loved him very much and she would take him back on one condition, which was that she would never give him another chance. Adam was overjoyed and promised that he would drink less.

Adam was as good as his word and drank a lot less. In his new position in the company, he would work a lot less hours, so he was able to eat with Maria almost every day. He was also determined to work very hard to have more quality time with Maria. They dined out a lot and they went to see musicals and operas. They also promised themselves that they would take two luxury holidays every year.

Meanwhile, Suzie had been feeling very guilty since the dinner. She thought that it was a harmless prank and she never intended it to go this far.

The next time that Suzie saw Adam, she confessed that she had lied to him and that they had not done anything together. Adam was relieved, but he berated her for lying in the first place and for spreading her lies around the office. He also said that she had almost cost him his marriage. Adam left Suzie in tears and drove back to his wife.

He was so eager to share the good news with his wife that he drove back much too quickly. He wasn't involved in any accident, but he must have left a few behind.

When he reached home and told Maria the good news, she was naturally delighted to learn that her husband had not, in fact, been unfaithful. However, she asked him how he could have put himself in such a vulnerable position. Adam did not want to answer. He still felt a bit guilty, because although he had not been unfaithful, the intent had been there. He held her and said, 'I am so very sorry'. He then kissed her tenderly and held her oh so tightly.

Maria had never been able to resist Adam's

embraces, so she felt all residual anger melting away. She was left with only one thought, 'at this moment I feel more contented, and safe than I have ever been'.

Adam and Maria had a long and happy life together. Of course, they had their share of arguments like most married couples, but they always managed to resolve their differences before they went to sleep.

Maria's Grandmother used to say, 'never go to sleep angry'. It was an old saying, but it was still appropriate for them. In fact, it works to this day.

The frustrated housewife

Emma had been happily married to Bill for twenty years. She had never been unfaithful to him in that time and nor was she likely to. But she did like to fantasise about being made love to by a handsome, virile, young man half her age. She suspected that the reason why she fantasised so much was that she was tired of the sheer tedium and repetitive nature of daily housework. It seemed to Emma that each boring week was exactly the same as the previous one, she would tidy up the house every day and she would do the dusting every other day, she would do the vacuuming twice a week and the polishing once a week. As for the ironing she would only do it when the pile of clothes was very high. It seemed that if she did a great deal of ironing and reduce the pile by a lot in a few days the pile was higher than before so if she managed to empty the ironing basket, in no time there it was full again.

She collected the milk from the doorstep and

saw that the milkman was long gone. A short while later the doorbell rang. She opened the door, and it was the postman who was very young and handsome, but he was also obviously gay, which didn't fit her fantasy at all.

About ten minutes later, the doorbell sounded again. This time a very handsome young man stood at the door. He announced himself as the gas engineer who was responding to her earlier call reporting a suspected gas leak. He gave his name as Andy and said that they took gas leaks very seriously, which was why he has come so quickly.

Emma showed Andy to the cupboard under the stairs where she first smelt the leak. He did not dare to switch on the light until the gas had cleared, so he used his torch instead. With the help of his 'sniffer', he located the source of the leak very quickly. He then told Emma that he would have to turn off the gas while he carried out a temporary repair. It was summer, she was not using the heating and she would not be needing the gas cooker until later, so she told him to proceed.

He told Emma that he had ordered the new part and would fit it as soon as it arrived. Once he had finished his work, he packed away his tools, relit the pilot light to the boiler and tested the cooker to see that all was well.

Meanwhile, Emma had finished tidying the

house. She had nothing else to do that day, so reluctantly she decided to tackle the huge pile of ironing.

She had just started the ironing when Andy entered the room, with his overalls removed down to his waist. He started to slowly unbutton his shirt and he said, 'Would you like me to do something to make you feel like a real woman?' Emma was so shocked that she went into one of her fantasies and was temporarily rendered speechless. Without thinking she nodded her head. He then removed his shirt and said, 'Are you sure that you want me to do something to make you feel like a real woman?' Emma thought that this was part of her fantasy, so she allowed herself to admire his perfectly sculpted torso and well-developed muscles and she said, 'Yes please!' as an automatic response.

Suddenly, Andy threw his shirt at her and said, 'Then run an iron over this will you!'. She was furious and in a fit of rage she hurled his shirt back at him, followed closely by the iron. Unfortunately, the iron was still plugged in, so as it dragged its plug out of the socket it reduced its speed through the air somewhat. This gave Andy just enough time to catch his shirt but dodge out of the way of the iron. Missing its intended target, it struck the window putting a large crack in it. The iron then dropped to the floor, breaking the casing and rendering it both dangerous and unusable. Andy made a hasty exit from the room before she threw something else.

He realised that he had out stayed his welcome, so he picked up his toolbox and ran out of the front door. He decided that when the part came in, he would ask one of his colleagues to fit it. After all, he dares not show his face there again.

Meanwhile, Emma was left to assess the damage. She knew that she could buy a new iron and it gave her a few hours to think of a suitable story to tell her Husband to explain the crack in the window, she was angry with Andy for leading her on but mostly she was ashamed of herself for temporarily confusing fantasy with reality. The only upside to this was that now she no longer had an iron, she couldn't do the ironing. Having no other choice, she reluctantly relaxed on the sofa to watch daytime television.

When she heard a key in the door, she knew it must be Bill, so she ran to the door to greet him. She threw her arms around his neck, kissed him passionately and gave him a tight hug, as if she were never going to let him go. He thought 'What a wonderful way to be welcomed home'. Emma grabbed him eagerly by the hand and led him upstairs, towards the bedroom.

After a particularly energetic half hour, Bill laid

on his back with a huge grin on his face. He was utterly exhausted, wide-eyed and totally bewildered but he was feeling rather pleased with himself. He stared at the ceiling thinking, 'I don't know what I have done to deserve this, but that was the best sex that we have ever had'.

Emma got up and started towards the door. She stopped halfway and said 'I am just going downstairs to make the dinner. If you want a shower, take your time and I will call you down when everything is ready'.

Downstairs the meat had been slow cooking in the oven and the vegetables had already been prepared and were sitting in cold, salted water. All she had to do was cook them and make gravy. Once everything was ready, she grabbed a bottle of wine and two glasses. She then called to her Husband, and they sat down to an intimate candlelit dinner, following which they relaxed on the sofa to watch a romantic movie.

After the film, Emma dragged Bill upstairs for an even longer session. Afterwards they both lay on their backs staring at the ceiling. Bill thought, 'I love you Emma, very much'. Emma thought, 'It is not so bad being a housewife. Fantasies are all very well, but there is no substitute for the real thing'.

The need for speed

From the age of about eight, Max showed a liking for going fast. He loved to ride on rollercoasters or anything which went fast. When faced with a decision whether to go in his Dad's car or that of his Uncle's, he would always choose his Uncle's. It is not because his Dad's was not a safe drive but because Max thought he was too slow. On the other hand, his Uncle was a very fast driver. One might say reckless.

Max's Dad knew that Max liked to go fast, but he had to find out if he was capable of driving fast. His Dad came up with the idea of encouraging Max to try driving go-karts.

Max did quite well at go-karting, so when he was ten his Dad enrolled him in a go-karting school.

Max turned out to be the model student because after only one year, he was doing all the maintenance and tuning on his karts. Also, he was finishing each race in the top three. Within two years, he was winning most races and his Dad felt that it was time to ask an agent to watch him race.

Things could not have worked out better for Max. Not only did he win his race, but he also crossed the finish line yards ahead of the rest. The agent was very impressed with Max's driving and skills, particularly for one so young. He said that with the consent of both Max and his Dad, he would take Max under his wing and find him a sponsor to put him through racing school. Papers were signed and within a couple of months the agent proved to be as good as his word and found Max a sponsor.

A month later, Max started at racing school. To start with Max wasn't very good, but once he had made the transition from a go-kart to a racing car, he started to do quite well.

After a year, Max was finishing in a podium position. After three years, he was consistently winning, and the agent thought it was time to move on, so he found a team in Formula three that were prepared to accept someone who was so young.

Max was delighted that, at the age of just sixteen, he would be a professional racing driver.

Four years went by with Max going from strength to strength. Then one day, he was head-hunted by a talent scout looking for a new driver for Ferrari.

The thought of driving in Formula one was a dream. Max found the transition to Ferraris quite easy and when the car had been customised to suit him, he drove quite well.

Of course, he had to get used to the considerable increase in power that the Ferrari had to offer. One thing which Max loved was its superb handling around corners.

One thing which was obvious from day one was that the only nemesis of Ferrari was Mercedes. Somehow the Mercedes engineers had been able to squeeze a bit more power from the engine, even though it was the same size as the one used by Ferrari. This meant that the Mercedes was able to overtake Ferrari on the straight parts of the track. Fortunately, the Ferrari had such superior handling that it was easily able to leave the Mercedes behind on the corners.

Max knew that his only way to beat Mercedes was to start in poll position and to somehow stay ahead until the first corner. On the next race, Max managed to secure poll position and he held Mercedes off by zigzagging on the first straight.

Max managed to put some distance between him and the Mercedes on the curved section of the track, but the Mercedes driver soon caught up with him on the next straight. He tucked in behind Max and after enjoying the benefits of being in the slipstream of the Ferrari, he pulled to the left and slingshot by. He meant to pull across just in front of the Ferrari, but unfortunately, he misjudged it and the Mercedes rear offside wheel collided with the near side front wheel of the Ferrari. The two wheels then locked, and the Mercedes tore off the Ferraris wheel. The two cars then began to spin. Having all four wheels intact, the Mercedes driver was soon able to regain control but having only three wheels, Max was unable to so anything to stop the Ferrari from spinning. It slammed into the crash barrier, removing both offside wheels. Now with only one wheel left, the Ferrari was just beginning to stop when it was hit by another car, which removed the one remaining wheel and sent the Ferrari chassis spinning faster than before. The chassis protected Max, as it was designed to do, and he was ok until it hit the crash barrier hard. This time there was an explosion, and the chassis was engulfed in flames.

Three track officials came to the rescue with one carrying a fire extinguisher which he used to douse the flames. Then the other two got Max out of the cockpit and carried him to safety. It was obvious that Max was in a bad way because the flames were so fierce that they had burnt through his leathers and had started on his fireproof suit. This is perhaps a misnomer because it should be called a fire-retardant suit. It had certainly saved his life, but it hadn't stopped him from being badly burnt.

The track officials phoned for an air ambulance and Max was air lifted to hospital. As soon as he arrived, he was taken straight to the intensive care unit (I.C.U.) in order to assess the extent of his injuries. When they had finished cutting off what remained of his fire-retardant suit, they discovered that he had sustained 80 percent burns to his body and when they carefully removed his helmet and balaclava, they found that he had sustained 50 percent burns to his head and face.

He was not expected to live, but he did. Max didn't have enough good skin left to do all the necessary skin grafts, so they had to clone his skin. This took a very long time, so several months of painful skin grafts later, he was finally transferred from the I.C.U. to a general ward.

When he was deemed fit enough, he started a course of physiotherapy to teach him to walk again and to control the rest of his muscles.

Finally, he was ready to be discharged and he surprised everyone by saying that he couldn't wait to race again. He spent several more months building up his muscles. He then returned to Ferrari. They didn't really want to take him back, but they felt obliged. The boss of team Ferrari had no great expectations for Max, so he didn't quite know what to do with him. Eventually, he made Max the first reserve driver. Even as a reserve driver, he was entitled to his own car, customised to his exact requirements. As soon as his car was ready, Max went out onto the track.

From the moment he started to drive, Max felt at home and within three months he was posting lap times which were faster than Ferraris best driver.

The boss was hugely impressed with Max's performance, not to mention rather shocked, so he scheduled Max for the next race. This would be Max's first race since his crash. Max was also told by one of the mechanics that's the engineers had squeezed as much power from the engine as they could, and they had reduced the weight of the body work as much as they dare without compromising the structural integrity of the car. This resulted in a car slightly slower than the Mercedes on the straight but much faster on the corners. It filled Max with the hope that he could defeat the giant.

On the day of the race, the weather was both warm and dry and it was forecast to remain so for the entire day. With virtually no chance of it raining during the race, all the cars had been fitted with slick tyres.

Max loved slicks because they complimented the natural handling of the Ferrari, and they suited his driving style. During the qualifying round Max excelled himself and recorded the fastest lap time. Consequently, Max started the race in poll position with a Mercedes in second position.

As soon as the starter light turned to green, Max blasted off the line like a thing possessed with the Mercedes in hot pursuit. On the pretext of further warming up his tyres, Max zigzagged just enough to stop the Mercedes from overtaking.

As soon as he reached the curve section of the track, Max was in his element, and he attacked each bend driving as fast as he possibly could. He pulled away from the Mercedes so that it was impossible for the Mercedes to catch him on the next straight, especially as it had lost most of its speed advantage.

The race consisted of several laps and Max continued to improve his lead on every lap. By the time Max had reached the halfway point, he had noticed that the car had developed a small fuel leak and by the time he had started the last lap he was running on fumes.

Also, he was starting to feel severe pain from his many skin grafts. They said that his new skin fitted him like a glove. At that moment, it felt like it was two sizes too small.

Max had a fair lead over the others, but he dares not stop for fuel. Instead, he carried on driving praying that the fuel would last until the end of the race. Sadly, it did not. The car spluttered to a halt, just a few yards from the finish line.

Max's rush of adrenalin temporarily masked his pain. He was acutely aware that his lead was rapidly being eroded, so he leapt out of the cockpit and pushed the car over the finish line. He had just taken the chequered flag before the Mercedes caught up with him. The feeling of elation reminded Max of when he was a child and won his first go-kart race. However, this feeling was much stronger, because he had just won his first formula one race.

Following an appeal by team Mercedes, a steward's enquiry was rapidly convened in order to rule on the legality of winning a race by pushing your car over the line. After due consideration, they ruled in Max's favour and upheld his win. Now that Max's win had been confirmed, it meant that Ferrari had taken first and third places with Mercedes in second place.

Max decided to wear his cap to the awards ceremony to hide his partial loss of hair. He climbed onto the podium, then, despite his facial disfigurement, he stood proud to receive his winner's trophy, the laurel wreath and the mandatory huge bottle of champagne. While Max was spraying the crowd with champagne he thought, 'this is the best moment of my entire life'. He also thought of the excruciating pain which he felt throughout the final lap, and he decided that this might be the time to retire. His Dad used to tell him 'Always leave the crowd wanting more'. Max considered it much better to go out on a high, rather than wait to fade out into relative obscurity. Besides, he was confident that at least in the first year, he would receive a lot of money from sponsorships, merchandise, personal appearances and other media options. After that, he was sure that several doors would open to him.

Max knew that Ferrari would take a while to find a replacement who would drive to the same calibre, but he decided that, for the first time in this life, he would start looking after number one.

His father's son

When Phil was just a mere toddler, he was close to both his parents. When he went to primary school, he became closer to his father. This was mainly because his Father worked from home and therefore was able to take him to school every day. Also, his Father used to help him with all his homework.

When Phil reached secondary school age, he developed a taste for sports. He also had a lot more homework. His Father continued to help him with his homework, and he encouraged his son in all his many sports. He would come to support Phil for all the major matches, and where possible, he would practise with his son in sports such as football, cricket, tennis and golf.

Of course, all of this came at a price. Phil wasn't allowed a mind of his own. His Father had mapped out his whole life and Phil dare not argue. When Phil had to choose his O-Level subjects his Father told him what to choose. When Phil received the results of his O-Levels, his Father was delighted to see that Phil had got an A grade in maths.

Phil decided that he would like to take four A-Levels. He was allowed to choose the number, but his Father chose the subjects. He then explained the career he had planned for Phil. This was a career as an investment banker. Phil complained bitterly because he had a passion for the arts. His Father explained that investment banking was a very secure career and if he showed a flair for it, it could be very lucrative. On the other hand, the arts were nothing more than hobbies, not careers. Phil knew that there was no point in arguing anymore, so he resigned himself to following his Fathers advice.

When Phil had completed the first year of his A-Levels, his Father encouraged him to apply to Oxford university, in order to read finance. His predicted grades were three B's and a C, and on this prediction, Oxford accepted him. One of Phil's grades was better than expected because he got an A in maths, so he went to Oxford.

Phil enjoyed university life immensely with only one reservation. Some of the boys who had the benefit of a private education regarded him as somewhat inferior, so Phil worked extra hard to prove them wrong.

Phil appeased his predilection for the arts by joining the university amateur dramatic society. With them, he appeared in many of their plays which he thoroughly enjoyed. Phil worked and played very hard at university and before he knew it, the three years were over. He left Oxford with a first-class honour's degree.

With a first from Oxford, Phil was surrounded by prestigious financial companies all competing to give him a job. After due consideration, he chose the one which seemed to offer the best package.

After Phil had started his new job, one of the senior consultants took him under his wing and, for the first two weeks, he learned the rudimentary aspect of the job. Within a month, he was showing a lot of promise. He also found out that he was enjoying the job much more than he thought he would. After three months he was doing very well and within one year he had made a great deal of money for both his many clients and himself. His clients tended to stay with him because he seemed to have the Midas touch and rarely made a mistake. When his shares did go down, they usually rallied within a couple of days and went higher than before.

Phil carried on working for several years, making a lot of money. Then he heard that his Father had contracted pancreatic cancer. The prognosis was not very good. Not only was it inoperable, but it was probably terminal.

Within a few months Phil's Father was gone. He was, of course, devastated by the loss of his Father, particularly because they were so close. One positive thing that came out of this tragedy was that now Phil was free to pursue his own destiny. He would keep doing his main job in order to pay the bills, but he would reduce his hours to three days a week and he would enrol at an art college.

After a respectful period of mourning, he approached the boss and said 'Although I love my job, I would like to reduce to three days a week. I would like to work from home for two of those days at the weekend and come into the office on Monday's'. The boss was reluctant to agree to the revised hours, but Phil was one of his best people, so he didn't want to lose him. Therefore, he agreed to the hours which Phil wanted.

Phil approached several art colleges until he found one that would accept him for only four days a week. For the next few months Phil tried various art forms including woodwork, metal work, textiles, sculpturing, painting and pottery, but he found that his passion lay in painting. More specifically he enjoyed painting landscapes in watercolour.

He knew that during term time, he would be

working seven days a week, but it didn't matter to him because he didn't regard painting as work. Anyway, he currently did unpaid work most weekends and this would be only for three years.

From the moment that Phil started to paint, the tutor could see that his work showed a lot of promise, so she encouraged him as much as she could.

Phil came on in leaps and bounds and by his last year, the tutor thought he was ready to sell his work. She looked around and found him some space in a local exhibition.

To Phil's utter surprise, he sold one of his paintings for £1,000. Spurred on by his success, he started to paint a lot more.

Even when he left art college, he continued to improve exponentially and the last time he exhibited he was selling his paintings for up to £3,000 each.

After a few years, his paintings had developed a following and were selling for up to £10,000. At this point, he decided to rent his own shop in which he displayed all his paintings.

He continued to thrive and one day he decided to quit his other job. After all, he was making enough money from his business.

Phil's business had gone very well since he opened the shop, so he decided to avail himself of the government backed scheme to take on an apprentice. He interviewed several candidates, each of whom brought samples of their work. All the paintings were good, but one young girl named Tina, produced work that showed a lot of raw talent. So, it was because of that Phil took on Tina for a two-year apprenticeship.

Most of their tea breaks were taken in the shop, but if they were working very hard and needed a longer break, Phil would shut up shop and treat Tina to a designer coffee at the local coffee shop.

Phil continues to impart all his knowledge to Tina, and he left the rest to her natural talent.

Within a year of her starting her apprenticeship, Phil considered her paintings to be eminently sales worthy, so he made some wall space for her to display her best pieces. He was delighted when she sold her first painting for £500. He was entitled to some commission on the sale, but he didn't need the money and he felt that he had done very little. Besides, she deserved to keep all the money.

Now that they had something to celebrate, Phil locked up early and took Tina to a wine bar. After a few glasses of wine, Phil started to relax, and he plucked up the courage to ask Tina out. Without hesitation, she accepted and added 'Why did it take you so long?'. She knew that he fancied her, and she had been waiting a long time for him to ask her out.

He couldn't answer at first, because he was too embarrassed. Finally, he said that he always seemed to be working much too hard to even think about socialising. She felt sorry for him. After all, he was nearly thirty and this would probably be his first date. She continued by saying that it was important for everyone to maintain a healthy balance between work and play. Phil knew that she was right, so he made himself a promise that if the first date went well, he would make it a regular occurrence.

The date went very well, so he kept the promise to himself and took her out at least twice a week.

Phil continues to teach Tina about painting, and she carried on improving. She also organised Phil's office for him because it was in dire need of it. She knew that he was an excellent artist, but he was completely disorganised. By the time she had finished reorganising his office, it looked neat and tidy, and she had put a system in place. This was in complete contrast to the shambolic state in which she found it.

After Tina had finished the office, she started to help Phil to re-paint the entire shop and to rearrange all the pictures. The shop, with its new facelift, proved to be very popular among his many visitors. Of course, most of the visitors only came to view the paintings, but occasionally a wealthy collector bought one of his more expensive pictures. If he sold one of his pictures each month, he was happy, but sometimes he sold two or even three. He also added some smaller works, which were much less expensive. These were much more popular and sold in great numbers. Most of them were bought by visitors who only intended to look but found his paintings irresistible.

By this point, Phil found Tina indispensable, and he could not imagine how he ever coped without her. When the apprenticeship came to an end the government would withdraw their funding, so Phil was determined that he would pay Tina a generous wage. Tina had always intended to leave as soon as her apprenticeship ended but she was happy in the job, so she decided to stay. The real reason was that her feelings for Phil were growing.

One day, Phil decided to auction his biggest and best painting, just to see what it was worth, so he gave it to the local auction house with a reserve price of £12,000. He was astonished when it sold for £30,000. Even after he had paid the commission and tax, it would still leave a lot of money.

This recent sale made him think of his Father and the drive and determination he had instilled in him, together with the work ethic and the sound business sense.

Phil knew that without all of these, he couldn't have come this far. However, there comes a time in everyone's life when they must be allowed to follow their own destiny.

Phil was sure that his Father would approve of Tina, because there wasn't anything not to like about her. He hoped that his Father would be proud of the way he had turned his 'hobby' into a thriving business.

Till death us do part

Zoe and Matt first met at a dance. Matt was beginning to doubt the wisdom of coming to a dance on his own, when he spotted Zoe standing on the opposite side of the room. She was wearing a dress which accentuated her curvaceous body.

Matt was attracted to her body, but he also found her quite beautiful. He decided to move in to take a closer look. When he reached her, he introduced himself, bought her a drink and they talked for nearly an hour.

Conversation came very easily to them both, so he asked her to dance. They danced for the rest of the evening. Before the evening ended, Matt asked Zoe to go out with him. Zoe found Matt attractive, so she had no problem accepting him.

The first date went very well, so it became a regular thing.

After a few months Matt found that he was falling in love with her, so he bought her a ring and proposed, just hoping she felt the same. Fortunately for Matt, Zoe had loved him for some time, so she said yes without hesitation.

They agreed that because they were both renting, their priority should be to save for a deposit on a house. The wedding would therefore be a simple affair at a registry office. When the day arrived, Zoe insisted on wearing a wedding dress and Matt wore a suit and tie. Apart from that, the wedding was far from traditional. They only had their two best friends there, to act as witnesses. And they chose the words for their vows. They also had no music.

They didn't even tell their parents that they were going to get married, until after the event.

Three of them took it quite well, but Zoe's mother was not happy. As Zoe was the only daughter, she had missed her chance to organise a big wedding. However, she soon came around when they took all the parents for a nice dinner.

The marriage seemed idyllic for the first ten years, with neither of them being even tempted to stray. They were just thinking that they had dispelled the theory that said, 'Marry in haste and repent at leisure', when their marriage started to unravel.

It started with them not talking very much to each other. Then Matt started to work late every day, so they rarely ate together. Even at weekends, he would shut himself away in their bedroom and would work on his laptop all day. At dinner time, he would order a takeaway for one.

They both knew that the marriage was over when he moved into the spare bedroom. Zoe was optimistic and was sure that one day soon their marriage would be back to normal.

However, this unhappy state of affairs continued for three long years and one day, Matt decided to finish work a bit earlier than usual and to stop at the local pub for a quick drink. After settling himself at his favourite table, he noticed a beautiful lady sitting on her own by the bar. She was looking quite sad, so he went to her to try and cheer her up. He asked what was troubling her and reluctantly she said that she had been stood up.

Matt wondered what sort of idiot would stand up such a beautiful woman; he was about to find out. Matt saw that her glass was nearly empty, so he bought her another drink. They talked until closing time, then he walked her home. He resisted the urge to invite himself in, but he did ask her for a date.

The first date was very good, but the second date was a complete contrast. At one stage during the second date, she went crazy for no reason, and it took all his strength to restrain her. The next date was the same, so Matt decided not to see her again. She was obviously in urgent need of some psychiatric help, so he chose not to get involved.

Fortunately, she didn't have his address for either work or home. The only phone number she had was his mobile and he was able to block her number.

Matt couldn't understand how he could possibly have been unfaithful to his wife with such a person, however bad the marriage was. The following day, he would be home early, so they could eat together. That evening Zoe prepared a lovely meal and she hoped that this would be the start of them saving their marriage. Unfortunately, Matt had other plans and nothing else changed. He still slept in the spare room.

One fine summers day, Matt decided to take a proper lunch break for a change, and he went for a long walk around the park. While strolling in the park, he saw a young lady coming towards him. She was using a handkerchief to wipe her eyes, as if she had been crying or had a bad case of hay fever. When she reached him, she dropped her handkerchief and they both bent down to pick it up. In doing so, they bumped heads and as they arose, their eyes met. As Matt looked into her deep brown eyes, he thought 'This is the one'.

With her permission, he did an about turn and

walked with her. As they walked, they talked a lot and he discovered that her name was Anna, she was twenty-four and she was single. She also said that she had no current boyfriend. This last piece of information was entirely unnecessary, but he took it as a welcome encouragement.

In due course, she had to get back to the office, but before she left, they exchanged numbers. On his way back to the office he was walking on air, and he felt like a boy again. Learning from mistakes of the past, he was determined to take this one very slowly. He left it a few days, then her phoned her one morning to ask if she would be going to the park at lunchtime. She said she was, so they arranged to meet.

Matt may have taken things too slow, because after two weeks, she was beginning to wonder if he would ever ask her out. She need not have worried, because a few days later Matt asked if she would consider going out with him. Trying not to look too keen, she said she would.

They dated for several months, then one day Matt said that he was married but his marriage had been a sham for the last four years. Anna was so shocked at hearing this and she said that she had seen a white mark on his wedding ring finger but had assumed that he was divorced. Matt said that he was going to ask his wife for a divorce, and he asked Anna if she would consider going on a short notice holiday with him. She said that with his revelation that he was still married, it had given her a lot to digest so she would need a couple of days to think about the holiday.

Meanwhile, Matt surfed the net and looked for last-minute deals in several travel agent's windows. He waited for two days before phoning Anna. He apologised for phoning so soon, but he wondered if she had reached a decision regarding the holiday. Anna said that she would love to go on holiday with him, if he had instigated divorce proceedings by then. Matt said that if he moved quickly, he could secure a fourteen-day holiday in the Caribbean in just three weeks' time. As for the divorce, he would speak to Zoe in the next couple of days.

The following morning, Matt told his wife that he would come home for dinner because he had something to tell her. She hoped it would be to discuss saving their marriage, but she was about to be disappointed.

That evening Zoe prepared a sumptuous meal and afterwards Matt said, 'As you know, we haven't been getting on at all well for four years, so I would like to finalise things by getting a divorce'. For a few seconds she was speechless. Then she said, 'Over my dead body!'. She was only speaking metaphorically, but she was signing her own death warrant.

Matt knew that without her consent, he would have to wait for four years before he could even file for divorce. He was not prepared to wait that long, so he had to think of another plan.

Matt knew that Zoe took a sleeping pill every night, so when he was in the bathroom, he looked for the bottle. When he found it, he made a mental note of the name. The following day at work, he researched the name online and discovered that when a 400mg tablet was taken every day, it was an effective cure for insomnia. However, it gave the stern warning that this dose should never be exceeded. It said that two tablets would make the person oversleep and they would awake with a terrible headache and a feeling of nausea. Three tablets would certainly prove fatal.

After about a week, Matt told Zoe that he would be in for dinner. During dinner, he told Zoe that he had met someone else, and he didn't want her to continue to feel like the co-respondent. He appealed to his wife to reconsider the divorce. However, Zoe was even more determined than ever that she would never agree to one.

After Zoe had retired to bed, Matt went into the bathroom and took two of her sleeping pills. Then he went to the kitchen and took the mortar and pestle. Once he was safely in his room, he ground one of the tablets into powder and poured it onto a piece of paper which he folded into a parcel and put it in his pocket. Then he did she same with the other tablet.

The day before the holiday, Matt told his wife that he would again be home in time for dinner. He said that he had been doing a lot of thinking about their previous discussions and as she was adamant that she would never give him a divorce, he had decided to try to save what was left of their marriage. She was delighted to hear this, little knowing that she would never live to see it.

That evening, shortly after the first course, Zoe went to the kitchen to fetch the main course. When she was gone, Matt poured her a glass of wine and into it he added the first lot of powder. He kept the two tablets separate in the hope that Zoe wouldn't taste it.

When Zoe returned with the main course and had taken her first sip of wine, she asked Matt if the wine tasted ok to him. He said that it tasted fine and added that it must be something she ate earlier.

Halfway through the main course, the phone rang and because her glass was nearly empty, he poured her another and added the second lot of powder.

When Matt was sure that Zoe was ensconced in

her room, he was sure that when she took her normal sleeping tablet, she would be effectively giving herself the fatal dose.

Matt then phoned Anna to tell her that something had cropped up at work which would need his urgent attention in the morning. He would therefore meet her at the airport.

It took Matt a long time to get to sleep. He regretted what he had done, but he knew that it was the only way he could ensure a future with Anna.

In the morning, he was not surprised to find that Zoe was not up, so he decided to finish his packing. He then ordered a taxi to take him to the airport.

Anna and Matt met at the airport as arranged and they flew off to the Caribbean for their two-week vacation. The first week was idyllic and they both enjoyed it immensely.

Meanwhile, back in the UK, Matt and Zoe's next-door neighbour was getting a bit anxious because she hadn't seen either one of them for three days. She rang the doorbell, but there was no answer. Finally, she opened the door with her spare key and cautiously entered the flat. When she opened the door to the main bedroom and saw Zoe's dead body, she screamed loudly enough for all the other flats to hear. Then, she broke down and sobbed. When she had recovered from the initial shock, she phoned her local police station and told them what she had found.

Two detectives arrived, and when they had seen the corpse, they phoned for the coroner. The body was taken away to have an autopsy performed. They found sleeping solution in the blood stream, which was three times the recommended dose. Taking two pills could be an accident, but taking three had to be intentional, so it was either a suicide or murder.

Back in the sunny Caribbean, Matt thought it was time to take the relationship to the next level and to do that, he would have to be entirely honest with Anna. He told her that he had asked Zoe for a divorce, but she was determined not to grant him one. He was then faced with no other choice but to kill her.

Anna was completely incredulous that he could be so callous, so she ran into the bedroom to pack. Matt tried to explain that it was the only way to ensure their future together. Anna replied, 'Now I have seen you in your true colours, we have no future together'. Anna stormed out to look for another hotel.

Three days later, she phoned him to say that she had found another hotel and she had extended her holiday by one day so she would be returning on a different flight.

Anna took another couple of days, thinking long and hard about what should be her next course of action. She did not want to involve the police, but felt it was inevitable and she wanted them to be in possession on the truth. Also, she was a firm believer that no crime should go unpunished. She thought that Matt was seriously disturbed and in need of help rather than incarceration.

She asked the local operator to connect her to 999 in England. When she got through, she asked to speak to her local police station. Once she had explained the nature of her call, she was put through to the murder squad. After she had told them about Matt's confession, they said that they were aware of the case, which was being investigated by the serious crime squad and they had been looking for Matt. They were keen to interview Matt, in the hope that he could assist them with their enquiries. However, they were unsure whether to treat the case as a suicide or a murder. The detective speaking to her added that now, with the information she had given him, the murder squad would be assuming control of the case.

On the last day of the holiday, Matt made his way to the airport. He waited, hoping that Anna would have had a change of heart and meet him there. When she didn't arrive, he boarded the plane on his own.

When the plane landed in England, he collected his luggage, passed through customs and entered the arrivals lounge. There he was met by two detectives, who arrested him on suspicion of murder.

The following day, Anna boarded her plane. She was sad because she thought that what was an ideal relationship with Matt, was now over. She also felt that the nightmare was also over – or was it?

Anna's plane landed safely and as she passed into the arrivals lounge, she was greeted by a detective, who offered to drive her home. On the way, the detective asked her if she would consider testifying at Matt's trial. Although she was reluctant to do so, she knew that it was the right thing to do, so she agreed.

At the trial, Anna gave her testimony, never daring to look at Matt. Largely thanks to her testimony, Matt was found guilty of pre-meditated murder and was sentenced to life imprisonment. The judge recommended that he should serve some of his time in a psychiatric ward.

Anna never felt able to visit Matt in prison, because she had been instrumental in putting him there.

In time, Anna found her Mr Right. They married and had three adorable children.

Meanwhile, Matt spent the rest of his life being bounced between prison and a secure psychiatric ward. His biggest regret was that he had lost the only two women who he had ever loved.

No smoke without fire

Amy was only five years old when she started to display an aversion to cigarette smoke, so it was inevitable that she would grow up to be a non – smoker. What was a complete surprise was that by the age of just ten, she had become an anti-smoker.

This was very unfortunate because her father was a very heavy smoker. This caused a substantial rift between them. It was a rift which would never truly be healed.

In the years running up to her tenth birthday, things got progressively worse. Whenever she went on a journey in her fathers' car, she had to keep asking him to stop, so she could get out to be sick. She always thought that she suffered from car sickness, but as time moved on, she noticed that she was never sick in anyone else's car. She then realised that it was her father's smoking making her sick, not the car. If her father wasn't smoking in the car, she would sleep peacefully on the back seat. However, if he suddenly started to smoke, she would wake up feeling nauseous.

If her father smoked indoors, he could fill the room with smoke. On the rare occasion that he wasn't smoking Amy would get engrossed in something on the television, but if he started smoking, she would stand up and leave the room, banging the door behind her.

She had just turned fifteen, when her older brother contracted terminal lung cancer, due to his heavy smoking. Lying in bed, he asked her if she had ever smoked and when she said no, he told her to never start. He went on to say that it was the easiest thing in the world to start, but the hardest thing in the world to stop. He said that he had given up smoking weed with relative ease, but he was totally addicted to smoking cigarettes. Even though he knew that the cigarettes were killing him, he couldn't stop smoking them.

A few weeks later he was dead. Amy was mortified because, although he was twenty-seven and there were many years between them, she had always felt close to him.

Her father was also devastated, having lost his oldest son and it made him look at his own habit. He tried everything he could think of to give up smoking, but everything failed. He tried gum, nicotine patches and even hypnotherapy and acupuncture but he found that the last two did nothing and he got addicted to the gum and the patches. He was able to cut down and he took great pride in telling his best friend that he had reduced his smoking to just forty cigarettes a day. Of course, this was only the packet cigarettes. He also smoked twenty roll ups a day.

When Amy was eighteen, she invited a boy to her parent's house to have a meal. She knew that he was a smoker, but she invited him anyway because she found him very attractive. She did tell him that he wasn't allowed to smoke in the house.

When Amy told her parents that she had invited a young man for dinner, they took it very well and arranged to go out for the evening. This would give her some privacy to entertain him.

On the day that he was due to come her mother spent all day tidying and cleaning the house, including putting away all ashtrays. Just before they went out, she went around the whole house with an air freshener, to mask the acrid smell of stale smoke. She paid particular attention to the lounge, where her husband did most of his smoking.

When Tim arrived, Amy could smell smoke on his clothes and breath. She invited him in and said that as it was such a warm evening, they would be eating outside. She had already laid a table on the patio complete with tablecloth, napkins and candelabra.

Amy had prepared a sumptuous three course meal for them, and she looked forward to a lovely evening.

As they were eating outside, Tim assumed it would be alright for him to smoke. Without even asking her, he lit his first cigarette. This proved to be the first of many, because he chain-smoked his way through the whole meal. This spoilt Amy's enjoyment of her meal and when she came to kissing him, she found it quite repulsive.

She didn't say anything after she kissed him, but her reaction spoke volumes. He got up and without saying anything, he left, and she never saw him again.

As she cleared the table, she reflected on what a disaster the evening had been.

Two years later, she had been getting on extremely well with her current boyfriend. She loved every part of him, especially because he was so considerate.

One day, he took her to the best restaurant that they had ever been to. Over a very romantic meal, he proposed to her. Of course, she accepted, without hesitation and she couldn't wait to tell her mother.

A year later, they were married, so she left the

family home and moved into their new love nest.

On the day of the wedding, she was very proud of her father because he didn't smoke throughout the service and when they all went outside, he was very discreet about his smoking and always wandered off on his own if he needed a cigarette. Similarly, at the reception, he refrained from smoking during the meal. After the meal, he always went outside for a smoke.

The first time that Amy's parents came to see the house, Amy explained to her father that it was a no smoking household and if he wanted to smoke, he would have to go outside. He seemed to take it well, but their subsequent visits were very infrequent.

One evening her father was smoking in his favourite armchair. There was nothing unusual about this, but what was out of character for him was that he fell asleep. He had been working extremely hard all day and he was exhausted. He should have gone straight to bed, but he had to have one last cigarette.

The cigarette set light to the arm of the chair and within seconds the whole chair was ablaze. It was a very old armchair and didn't comply with modern fire regulations. He didn't wake up before he passed away.

The fire spread to the rest of the room and

within a few minutes the whole of the ground floor was on fire.

Fortunately, mother was a light sleeper, so when smoke from the fire crept up the stairs and into her bedroom, she woke up. She put her on her dressing gown and went downstairs to investigate.

She opened the lounge door and saw it was too late to save her husband and that the whole of the ground floor was on fire. She quickly shut the lounge door and left the house by the front door.

She stood in the front garden and wept for her husband. She then watched in disbelief as the whole house went up in flames.

One of the neighbours phoned for the fire brigade, but by the time they arrived, they were only in time to save the house, not the contents.

Fortunately, they were well insured, and the insurance company put her up in a hotel while the house was being renovated. They then replaced all the contents so she could move back in.

Amy had just celebrated her thirty-first birthday, when she was told that her father had perished in a house fire. Although she had never been close to her father, she sobbed uncontrollably, because it was her father. Also, he was only sixty-six and far too young to die.

When Amy reached her fiftieth birthday, she suddenly realised that in the last decade, she had not met one smoker who didn't want to quit, so the obvious question was, 'why start in the first place?'

It was probably the fault of successive governments who had taken no action against the cigarette companies, because they raised a lot of tax from the sales of cigarettes. They never even stopped allowing the cigarette companies to advertise, glorifying the smoking of cigarettes.

These adverts mainly targeted males, saying that you were not a real man unless you smoked. They assumed that all females would be introduced to cigarettes by their husbands or boyfriends.

Amy understood why people of her father's generation would have started smoking. After all, when he was younger, nothing, was known about the harmful effects of smoking. Not only was the habit not discouraged, but it was also actively encouraged. If you were in the army, part of your pay was in cigarettes and some doctors would recommend smoking to pregnant women as a means of helping them to calm down.

As a result, 60 % of the entire population smoked. If you were a non-smoker, you were in the minority and you were made to feel decidedly odd. However, now she couldn't understand why anyone would start smoking, because so much was known about its harmful effects on your health and the addictive nature of nicotine.

Eleven years later, in order to mark the occasion of their ruby wedding anniversary, Tim and Amy hosted a big party. It went very well, and a good time was had by all. Unfortunately, Uncle Sid had a bit too much of a good time and drank far too much. He became rather unsteady on his pins and at one stage, he fell over, bringing down a lot of bottles on top of him. Only one of the bottles broke, but it made a great deal of mess. Luckily, his wife was on hand to take him home. They left in short measure, before he did any more damage.

The day before the party Tim surprised Amy by saying that he had booked a table for two, in the no smoking section of the most prestigious restaurant in their area.

When the day arrived, they approached the restaurant with great anticipation, but when they got there, they were very disappointed to find that the no smoking section consisted of one small table, surrounded by smokers. They immediately asked to be moved to a part of the restaurant, where no one appeared to be smoking. There was one empty table next to theirs, which they were quite grateful for.

They had just finished their starter and they were in the process of having their main course served when, three people came to occupy the empty table. Two of them seemed to be a couple, with their friend sitting opposite. Their hearts sank when they saw the friend put two packets of cigarettes on the table. He immediately took one of the cigarettes out, but to their amazement, before he lit it, he asked them if they minded him smoking. Amy was embarrassed, because they were in a smoking area, but she said, 'it is very kind of you to ask me, but I would prefer you to refrain from smoking while we are eating our main course.'

To their utter surprise, he stood up and went outside, taking a cigarette and his lighter with him. While he was gone Amy asked the couple what he would normally drink before dinner. They replied that he would usually have a pint of lager, so Tim ordered one to be brought to their table but added to his bill.

When he returned, he thanked his friends for the drink. They corrected him, by saying that it had been paid for by the other table, pointing at Tim and Amy. He tried to protest, saying that it really wasn't necessary. Amy said 'It is our pleasure. In my whole life, you are the most considerate smoker that I have ever met.'

To their further surprise, he did not smoke throughout their meal and every time he needed a cigarette he got up and went outside.

When Tim and Amy had finished their meal,

Tim had paid the bill and Amy had thanked the young man once more for his being so considerate, they left.

They had enjoyed a wonderful meal, in a smoke-free environment. They had accompanied their meal with a splendid claret.

Not long after the meal, Amy developed a cough and started to complain of chest pains. She should have gone straight to the doctor, but she delayed it. After two months she still had the cough, and the chest pains were worse. Also, she had started to develop a shortness of breath.

She went to the doctor, and he sent her straight to hospital. There, she was diagnosed with terminal stage four lung cancer. Within a few weeks, she was no more.

Nobody could understand how someone who had never smoked could get lung cancer. Tim had a theory that it had been caused by her inhaling the smoke of others, but he had no proof, so it remained just a theory.

Two years after she died, a scientist published a paper which said that he had established a direct link between non-smokers who inhaled the second-hand smoke of others and then contracted lung cancer. He called it,' Passive smoking.'

Tim was pleased that at last his theory had been proved right. As a direct result of this paper, the government was forced to act.

They made all restaurants become entirely no smoking and shortly after, they banned smoking in all public places. This included pubs, bars, cinemas, theatres and public transport. There was resistance against having no smoking in pubs and bars, but this soon dwindled.

The next move by the government was to ban adverts for cigarettes and to force all cigarette companies to put their cigarettes in plain packaging, emblazoned with the slogan 'smoking kills!'

A year later, a census was taken of the whole country, and it revealed that the number of people who smoked had plummeted to less than two per cent of the population.

Tim was happy that at last, he represented the majority, but he wished that his wife had lived to see this day.

In the name of the law?

Detective Sergeant (DS) Roy Wallander had been a policeman for twenty-seven years, so he was only three years away from retirement. He had taken the detective exam after nearly five years, and he had been promoted to Sergeant Just over ten years ago. He was transferred to a Serious Crime Squad, and he had been there ever since. Although they had introduced the rule of 'tenure,' a long time ago it was easily circumvented, by changing the job title, every two years. The rule of tenure was first introduced to prevent police officers from having a cushy office job, for more than two years.

The job of the Serious Crime Squad was to arrest high-profile criminals, who either; laundered large amounts of money, dealt in drugs, acted as pimps to more than twenty prostitutes, smugglers of diamonds and other precious gems, or got involved in any other serious crime.

DS Wallander answered to Detective Inspector (DI) Len Snyder when he was at the station but when he was on the street, he was completely autonomous. In fact, he had six young detective constables (DCs) working for him.

Roy had been admired for many years as a role model for new recruits to emulate. However, the thing that made him most proud was that for three years he held the record for the most arrests of any serious crime officer throughout the entire police force.

One day, when DS Wallander had arrested a major drugs dealer, he was on his way back to the station when the drug dealer offered him a substantial bribe to let him go. Roy knew that the right thing to do was to continue to the station, but the bribe on offer was more than he could earn in a year. Most officers were always complaining about their pay, but this was Roy's chance to do something about it. Therefore, he took the bribe and let the villain go.

Having crossed the line once, it was easy for Roy to continue to do so. Every month he would let one criminal go, in return for a very large bribe.

If Roy had carried on his nefarious activities at this level, he might have got away with it. However, Roy got greedy, and he started letting go of two or three criminals every month, in return for an equally large bribe. He also recruited three of his DCs to assist with his rather lucrative crime.

He told them how to suggest a bribe and how much to ask and in return he would take 20% of the money that they make.

The DI's attention was first drawn, when he noticed that DS Wallander was making a lot fewer arrests and that he no longer held the record for the most arrests. Also, one of his DC's was acting in a way that suggested that he had come into a lot of money.

THE other two conscripted DC's were more discreet about the bribery money and had transferred it all into a separate savings account. One DC had put most of the money into a savings account, but he kept some for spending.

One day the DC came to work, driving a flashy new car and wearing designer clothes and handmade shoes. The DI decided to interrogate him about his newfound wealth.

It didn't take long before the DC cracked and admitted that he had been taking bribes and he was charged with acting in a manner unbefitting an officer of the law. He was also charged with corruption.

When the case came to court, he was found guilty of both charges. However, the judge was lenient on him because he was young, he had an otherwise unblemished record and there was no conspiracy involved. The DC was given a two-year suspended prison sentence and he was told to serve two-hundred hours of community service. The Judge further ordered that all money obtained through bribery should be confiscated. The police force stripped him of the rank of detective, and he was transferred to another station. He was allowed to keep his clothes, but he would have to be pay for them from his own savings. The car was returned to the dealership, for whatever the dealer would give for it and the proceeds added to the officers' confiscated ill-gotten gains.

The DI was about to go after DS Wallander, when he was promoted to Detective Chief Inspector and sent to another station. During the briefing of his replacement, a DI Jack Cramer, he told Jack to keep an eye on DS Wallander.

After Jack had grown accustomed to his new job, he obtained a court order to examine the bank accounts of DS Wallander and all six of his DC's. As you would expect, the accounts of the new DC showed no irregularities and nor did the accounts of three of the other DC's. The two remaining DC's showed regular large deposits to their current accounts. The majority of the money was then transferred to a savings account and the rest was transferred to DS Wallander. On looking at DS

Wallander's account the DI discovered that several large amounts of money had been deposited into his current account, along with smaller amount transferred from the two DC's. No doubt this was some sort of commission.

All his ill-gotten gains were then transferred to a bank in Zurich. This was, no doubt an attempt to evade tax.

When Roy realised that he had been discovered, he slipped out of the office and went on the run. His first stop was to his flat. He knew that this would be the first place that they would look for him, so he made his visit brief. First, he phoned to order a taxi to take him to Heathrow airport, then he packed some of his clothes and a few essential items. He then hurried downstairs, to wait for the taxi.

Meanwhile, the DI interrogated the two corrupt DCs. Faced with indisputable evidence, they both confessed that they had been taking bribes and that this was organised by DS Wallander. They were both charged with conspiracy to pervert the course of justice and corruption.

Roy's taxi arrived and he headed for the airport. His aim was to fly to the States and to open a bank account there, transferring all his money from Switzerland.

DI Cramer was sure that Roy would attempt to

leave the country, so he contacted his superintendent and with his permission he deployed all his detectives to Heathrow and city airports, as well as Stanstead and Gatwick. DS Wallander had not taken his car, so it was possible to rule out the ferry or the euro tunnel, but the DI made sure to send two DCs to the departure point for the Eurostar.

The detectives at Heathrow managed to intercept Roy as he was about to board a plane for America. They arrested him for evading capture and took him back to the station. Once there, he was further charged with conspiracy to pervert the course of justice and corruption.

The DI took a further look at the current accounts of DS Wallander, but this time, he went back several weeks. The DI discovered that the first officer to be charged, had also been transferring money to the sergeant. The young officer was further arrested and charged with conspiracy and perjury, because he had sworn in court that he had been acting alone.

The court case was convened in record time and the officer was found guilty of both charges. Because it was found that a conspiracy had been involved, he was sentenced to spend two years in prison, instead of the two-hundred hours of community service, and for the perjury he was fined £1,000. He was subsequently dismissed from the police force without pension.

It was perhaps because the three remaining cases all involved corruption within the police force that the cases all came to court very quickly. Although the three cases were all heard separately, they all came to court on the same day. The two DC's were found guilty of both charges and were sentenced to spend two years in prison. Meanwhile, all the bribery money was confiscated, and they were dismissed from the force, without pension. The last part did not worry them too much because they were both young enough to find another job and to start a new pension.

When DS Wallander had his day in court, he was also found guilty of all charges, but because he was seen as the master mind, he was sentenced to spend four years in prison.

DI Cramer's only frustration was that the original court order only allowed him to access UK – based bank accounts, so he applied for another one to allow him to view Roy's Zurich account. When he looked at it, he was astounded to find that it contained nearly two million pounds. With the co-operation of Interpol and a Swiss judge, he was able to transfer all the money to the UK, for confiscation.

Roy knew that when he came out of prison, he

would be forty-eight. He was fairly confident that he could get another job, but a pension at that age would be very expensive. Also, he would be retiring much later than he expected.

Four long years gave Roy plenty of time to reflect on his misdeeds. He had spoiled an otherwise unblemished career. One thing that kept springing into mind was the saying: 'crime doesn't pay'!

Call this life?

It seemed to Jeff that from the day he was born his whole life had been just a series of unfortunate events, so he had decided to end it all.

Jeff was born six weeks premature and weighing only two pounds, so he spent the first few weeks of his life in an incubator.

He grew up as a scrawny and sickly child, so at junior school he was always bullied and had very few friends.

By the time he went to senior school he had filled out a bit and his health had been restored. However, he had no self-confidence, so consequently he still had very few friends.

He also found it very hard to mix with the girls. Later in life he developed acute acne. This was possible to control, but it left scars. This was yet another dent to his already battered confidence.

Every child has childhood illnesses, but Jeff had them all. He had measles, chicken pox, whooping cough, mumps, and German measles. It is said that if you have chicken pox once, you will never have it again. Instead, adults tend to get shingles. In Jeff's case, he got chicken pox a second time when he was twenty and he got shingles when he was thirty-five.

Jeff was not much interested in any of the subjects at school, except woodwork and music, so he did very little studying. Consequently, he left school with only two O levels, these being music and woodwork.

This rather precluded any chance that he might have had to go on to further education. It also limited his choice of jobs.

Finally, his uncle got him a job with his firm, working as a mail boy.

As well as delivering the mail twice a day, Jeff's responsibilities included making tea and retrieving files as necessary. He enjoyed the job, but it took him ten years before he was promoted to clerk.

When Jeff bought his first car, he got it from a dealer. He assumed that the dealer could be trusted, so he did not even think of employing an independent mechanic. This proved to be a big mistake, because the car developed many problems and eventually, he had to sell it. For his second car, he bought privately, and he took along a mechanic.

The mechanic found a few minor problems, which reduced the price, but overall, he said that it was a good car.

When Jeff reached the age of twenty-two he made the decision to leave the world of renting and to buy his very own house. As it would be his first purchase, he decided to buy a new build. Hopefully, he would not inherit the sort of problems which an older building might present. For the same reason, he also didn't bother with a structural survey. This proved to be yet another a big mistake.

In the first week, Jeff found no fewer than fourteen minor problems. He drew them to the attention of the builders, who were happy to fix them as they came under the heading of snagging. One week after the last problem had been fixed, Jeff noticed that cracks were starting to appear in one of the outside walls. These cracks grew rapidly bigger, so he showed them to the builder. This time, the builder was less than cooperative and said that there was nothing he could do and that it should have been picked up by the structural surveyor. Jeff knew that he hadn't instructed a structural surveyor, so he contacted his insurance company. They were prepared to pay for the underpinning, but he would have to pay the first £1,000. He could not afford such a large amount, so he was left with no option but to have it added to his mortgage.

Jeff stayed in the house for a few years after the work had been finished, but then he sold it, in favour of an older property. Because the price of structural survey was so high, he decided not to have one. This was a decision he would live to regret and very soon.

On the first day of moving in, he was taking some things up to the loft when he discovered considerable woodworm to some of the roof supports. Also, the roof was leaking in three places, where tiles were either broken or missing. He contacted his insurance company but there was nothing they could do, because it was a pre-existing problem. Jeff did the only thing he could do, and he got a roofer to do the work and add the money to his mortgage.

Jeff had never had a lot of luck with women, so he joined an online dating agency. He had several dates which didn't work out, then he finally met someone who he was instantly attracted to. After a few successful dates, he took Kim to meet his parents. They liked her straight away and his mother went as far as to say, 'this one is a keeper!'

Soon after, he discovered that she didn't work, neither did she want to work. Also, what Jeff didn't know was that Kim was a bit of a 'gold digger.'

What she didn't know was that Jeff was the wrong person to choose, because he didn't have any money. In fact, the only thing of any value which he owned was the house and that was mortgaged up to the hilt.

It was obvious, from the outset, who was going to wear the trousers in their relationship, as she chose where they would go and left him to pay. He could see that the relationship was not likely to last on that basis, but his mother put pressure on him to marry her.

He was never able to resist his mother, so he proposed to Kim.

The wedding was a simple affair, despite Kim's wishes. One thing which she did insist on was a decent honeymoon. She chose where they should go, and he had to pay.

When they returned from their honeymoon and Jeff started working, he looked forward to coming home to a spotless house and a home-cooked meal. However, he was disappointed to find Kim in front of the tv, having done nothing all day. This behaviour continued every day, and he was expected to do all the housework when he came home from work and then cook the dinner.

He put up with this for three long years, then against his beliefs and principles, he instigated divorce proceedings. It was only then that he realised that he had done a very wise thing in taking the solicitor's advice to get Kim to sign a pre-nuptial agreement. This made them tenants in common, entitling her to only twenty-five per cent of the equity in the house. This document would only be invoked in the event of a divorce. It was seen as more than fair, considering that she had not paid anything towards the deposit on the house and currently she contributed nothing towards the mortgage repayments. This would have been fine, if she had done any housework or cooking, but she did absolutely nothing, except watching tv all day.

Jeff had always told Kim that he could not afford to support her lifestyle, but she never believed him. Now, when she looked at the size of the cheque, she finally realised that he had no savings.

Jeff ended up living in a two-bedroom flat, which is all he could afford. Kim moved back in with her parents.

As if life had not been cruel enough to Jeff, he was diagnosed with cancer of the prostate. Fortunately, it was caught early enough to treat and in one year, he was declared in full remission.

In his mid-forties, he was coming down the stairs at home rather too quickly, when he tripped on a piece of loose carpet and fell the rest of the way. He landed awkwardly and broke both his arm and his leg. Both were easy to set, but he was hobbling around, for a few weeks.

The final straw came one fine, sunny afternoon, when the big boss asked to see Jeff in his office. This was never good news and it left jeff wondering what it was all about.

Jeff entered the boss's office and closed the door. The boss explained that the company had seen some hard times in the last few months, and he had decided to make a few people redundant. Although he was happy with Jeffs work, he wasn't as productive as the younger staff, so he had decided to let Jeff go.

When Jeff left the boss's office, he went straight to the gents. Once there, he sat down and wept. He had given the company thirty years of his life, and this was all he got as thanks.

He must have dozed off because when he went back in the open plan office everyone had gone home. He was now deprived of saying goodbye to anyone. He had been given a box to fill with his personal effects and he had been instructed to take his things and leave. He would be paid for the next month in lieu of notice then during this time he would receive his redundancy money. While he was looking at his belongings, he reflected on what a tragic life he had led, from the moment he was born. Then, in a moment of what can only be described as sheer insanity, he rushed to his nearest opening window and climbed out onto the windowsill. Fortunately, the sill was very deep and made of concrete, so there was little chance of him accidentally falling off.

The office was on the tenth floor, so when he glanced down, he saw it was a very long way to fall. He knew that no one could survive such a fall, so he had to be very sure that he wanted to go through with this. He then closed the window till it was just ajar. Then he stepped across to the other side of it and there he stood frozen to the spot, while he decided upon his next course of action.

He must have been there for about ten minutes because a crowd of people had gathered below, to watch the drama unfold. One man even had a video camera, to record the event.

At that moment police started to arrive and one of the sergeants told one of his WPCs to go up to the office. She was trained to persuade potential suicides to change their minds.

When WPC Liz Westlake stepped out of the lift on the tenth floor, she found his office and then looked for Jeff standing on the windowsill. When she found him, she cracked open one of the top windows, so Jeff could hear her. Then she proceeded to talk him down.

She seemed to be having a fair degree of

success, so when she saw that one of the main windows was already ajar, she decided to push it open wide, so that jeff could climb back in.

Unfortunately, she pushed it open with such force that it knocked Jeff off the windowsill, and he plunged to his death. Liz was in such a state of shock, that all she could think to say to herself was 'ooops!' soon afterwards, her radio crackled into life, and it was her sergeant ordering her back down.

When WPC Westlake reached the ground floor, her sergeant wasted no time in grilling her. 'What the hell just happened?' he said, 'I told you to talk him down not knock him down!' He then ordered her back to the station, where he would deal with her later.

When Jeff fell, the crowd gasped and the man with the camera filmed it.

Soon after Jeff fell, the inspector phoned for the coroner and when he arrived, he pronounced Jeff dead at the scene. He then carried the body to his car, saying that he was going to take him to perform an autopsy. None of the officers could understand why an autopsy was necessary, because it was obvious what had happened. What none of them thought of was the usefulness of a tox screen.

The tox screen showed a significant amount of a hallucinogenic drug in his blood, so this was probably why he stepped out onto the sill in the first place.

After further research, he discovered that only a week previously, someone had taken a blood sample from Jeff, which revealed that there were no drugs in his system, so this suggested that the drug had been administered by a third party.

It suggested murder, but as there was no proof or suspects, the police were prepared to take the matter no further. The coroner was left with no choice but to declare death by suicide.

This seemed very unfair to Jeff, but the police were under-resourced, so they were unable to take the matter any further.

The man with the video camera was able to film Jeff's descent, but he missed the start, when Jeff was knocked off the ledge. Consequently, he had nothing incriminating to send to the police. Liz was fortunate, because all she received was a dressing down by her sergeant and a blackmark on her record. However, she excused herself from any further involvement in potential suicide cases.

The coroner felt very frustrated by the police's inability to progress the matter, so he decided to impart his findings to all of Jeff's colleagues at the office.

One of Jeff's colleagues, called Sue, had her suspicions about one of the supervisors. He was called Ian Ogilvy and although he was a married man, he had been having an affair with one of the typists. Jeff had somehow found out about the affair and was blackmailing him. She decided to share her suspicions with the police.

Armed with this new information about possible suspects, they re-opened the case.

They raided Ian's house and confiscated his laptop.

Once they had his laptop back at the station, they looked at his emails, including the deleted ones. From these, they learned that he had indeed been having an affair and was being blackmailed by Jeff. With assistance from one of their computer wizards, they then went back to Ian's laptop to look at his history of internet searches. They soon found that he had been looking for, hallucinogenic drugs and he had placed an order for some.

Under fairly stringent interrogation, Ian confessed to killing Jeff.

At the court case, Ian pleaded guilty to the murder of Jeff Casey. He was sentenced to thirty years in prison.

This would not bring Jeff back, but it would vindicate him. He would not be remembered as the person who had committed suicide but as the victim of a murder.

So, you think you want to be a brain surgeon?

It was very early in the morning and was still dark when Sarah bounded out of bed. Her alarm had not yet gone off, but she was anxious not to miss the sunrise. The weather forecast for the day was fine, but more than that she was looking forward to her first day at school. Children have very different reactions to their first day at school, but Sarah was thoroughly excited. Her first day went extremely well and within a few days, her teacher had noticed that she was brighter than most of the other kids.

Two years later, Sarah went to junior school. She was determined to work hard in every subject and consequently came top in each exam. Fortunately for Sarah, she was also fairly good at sports. This gained her many friends and saved her from being labelled the class swot. When she sat her eleven plus exam, she did extremely well, guaranteeing her a place at the local grammar school.

Once at grammar school, she continued to work hard. This was not out of place at the grammar school, because everyone seemed to work hard. Her final qualifications were very good indeed and comprised twelve A grade O'levels and five A grade A 'levels. With such qualifications, she was able to take her pick of any of the universities.

Sarah had always wanted to be a doctor, so she decided to go to Oxford university, in order to study medical science.

She came away from Oxford, with a first-class honours degree. Armed with a degree like this, meant that the world was her oyster, but there was only one place that she wanted to go, which was medical school. She knew that she wanted to be a doctor, but she didn't yet know what sort.

Sarah had read a lot about the intricacies of the human brain and had come to realise how little was known. She decided at that moment that she wanted to become a neurosurgeon.

Sarah graduated from medical school and served as a general Doctor in a hospital, for a few years. Then she worked as a junior surgeon, assisting with one of the most prominent neuro-surgeons in the country.

She continued to work with him for many years,

learning a great deal. Finally, he moved on and Sarah was expected to fill his shoes. They were very big shoes to fill, so as the day of her first operation approached, she was very nervous, but she knew that she was ready.

The first operation went very well, and she carried on performing many successful operations, continually growing in both confidence and experience.

Then, one day, she woke up to find that she had been working for twenty-five years, performing hundreds of operations and she had never lost a patient. This was somewhat unique in the world of neurology. However, something was about to happen that would threaten her record.

Sarah was referred a patient, who was described as having an inoperable brain tumour. The tumour was malignant, so it was effectively handing the patient a death sentence. He had been seen by several neurosurgeons who had all agreed that the tumour was too imbedded in the brain to operate, without doing irreversible damage. Sarah looked at his MRI scan and made the decision that she could remove the tumour without damaging the brain. She realised that the operation would carry a great deal of risk, but the man's life was at stake, so she decided that it was a risk worth taking.

Surrounding herself with only the best

anaesthetist, junior surgeons and nurses, she performed the operation.

Having removed the top of the skull, she proceeded to cut out the tumour, with a laser scalpel and a great deal of skill. The operation had gone very well, and she had just handed over to one of the junior surgeons to close up, when the heart rate started to plummet. It went lower and lower, until it flat-lined.

She told one of the nurses to bring the defibrillator. The nurse did as she was told and charged it, setting it to the lowest voltage, before giving the paddles to Sarah. Sarah placed the paddles on either side of Leon's heart and pressed the button. There was no reaction, so Sarah asked the nurse to increase the voltage slightly and recharge the paddles. Sarah continued to apply a voltage to his heart, until she reached the full voltage, but there was still no sign of life. She was about to call the time of death, when she thought 'No, I refuse to give up! I have been operating for twenty-five years, without ever losing a patient, so I am not about to start now.'

Sarah started to give Leon a vigorous chest massage, after which she used the paddles twice more. Slowly Leon's heart started to beat. It was sporadic to start with, but it soon became more regular.

Once Sarah knew that he was out of danger, she breathed a sigh of relief, and she said a silent prayer of thanks.

Sarah had two golden rules, which she always adhered to. Firstly, she never referred to any patient by name and secondly, she never kept in touch with any of her patients. However, she had saved Leon's life, so she broke both of her rules and stayed in touch with Leon for many years.

Leon continued to make a full recovery and after he was discharged, he went on to lead a long and healthy life.

Sarah continued to work for another ten years and retired, still holding her record for having never lost a patient.

I have a cunning plan

Lee was under no illusion that he would ever be top of the class, but he was consistently in the top twenty-five percent

When the time came for him to sit his O-Levels, he passed them all, but only got one A grade. Similarly, he passed all three of his A-Levels but with no A grades.

Although he went to university, he was unable to go to his first choice.

Lee emerged from university with a respectable lower second-class honours degree.

He had always been good at organising and he excelled at planning. Therefore, it was no surprise that for his job, he became a project manager. All his projects finished on time and on budget, a fact of which he was most proud.

Lee continued to run projects, as if they were on rails. Then when he was in his mid-forties, he suffered a severe stroke which left him with what is known as locked in syndrome.

In his case, this meant that he was left paralysed from the waist down.

He spent the first few weeks feeling sorry for himself and thinking of all the things which he could no longer do. Then he thought 'This is getting me nowhere. It is time I started focusing on the things I can do.'

Lee knew that the best thing he could do was to plan something, but what?

Lee thought long and hard about what he should plan. Finally, he decided that the most daring thing he could do was a bank heist. This would be no ordinary bank. It would be the Bank of England.

Using his contacts, which he had built up over the years, Lee managed to obtain the plan, showing the storm drainage system, which ran under the bank. Also, he managed to get a plan of the bank and all surrounding buildings. He had this reproduced on a melonex sheet and to the same scale as the storm drainage system. By laying one on top of the other, you could easily see where to drill, to get into the vault.

Lee assumed that the front, back and sides of the bank would be impregnable, so he thought that he would come in from underneath. He then assembled a team of six people, all chosen for their specific skills. Tom was an expert in drilling large diameter holes. Harry was used to drilling out locks. Jake was experienced in dealing with alarm systems and Ben was a very good driver.

Of the two remaining members of the team, Tim was exceptionally good when he was working on a computer, particularly when he was hacking into various websites. Most of his work would be carried out in the weeks preceding the heist. Ivan had no specific area of expertise, but he was very strong, which Lee thought would come in very handy.

Lee rented a lock up for three months and he had it fitted with an ultra-fast internet connection and a telephone line. He then furnished it with a four-piece suite, to allow all of them to relax in comfort. He also bought a large table and chairs so that they could do the planning. Last of all, he bought a desk, operators chair, super-fast laptop and a telephone answering machine.

Having hired Tim, Lee got him to hack into the bank's website, In order to obtain plans of the vault, together with cross-sections of the construction. He was also able to ascertain which firm provided the security system and copies of the staff rota. Lee then asked Tim to hack into the security firms database, to find out what sort of system had been provided. Finally, Lee got Tim to hack into the environmental services website, to get cross-sections of the storm drainage ducts.

He then told Tom that he would have to drill through one foot of concrete plus three inches of solid steel, to get into the vault. The hole would have to be large enough for a big man to crawl through. Tom was convinced that he could do it, but he would need some specialized equipment. Lee gave the security details to Jake, for his information. Jake immediately noticed that the only security arrangements inside the vault were two cameras, so he asked Tim to hack into each camera and download and print a photograph of what they could see.

Also, Lee told Harry that he could expect to find a block of one hundred safe deposits boxes, and he provided details of the locks that had been fitted. This would help Harry to bring the right type of drilling equipment.

Lee then purchased a van which would accommodate six people. He then had added the details of a window cleaning company onto the side of the van. This was so a ladder on the roof would not look out of place. If anyone rang the number, a message would say 'we are currently experiencing severe staff shortages so we will not be taking on any new work.'

On the day of the robbery, Ben drove the other five to the bank and was careful to park around the corner. They then entered the storm drain, each carrying two large, empty bags and wearing a large rucksack. Ivan carried four bags, because of his superior size and strength.

Tom had marked on his plan the precise spot to drill to come up inside the vault. The team walked through the storm drain, until they reached the right spot.

While Tom started to drill through the concrete, Jake looked for the feeds to the two cameras. Once Tom had finished drilling through the concrete, Ivan helped him bring down the lumps of concrete. Before Tom started to cut through the steel, Jake cut the camera feeds. He knew that the cameras couldn't be left without feeds for too long, in case they were being monitored.

As soon as Tom had finished cutting through the steel, he positioned the ladder and climbed up into the vault. Unfortunately, someone had positioned a very heavy desk above the hole. Tom sent Ivan up the ladder to move the desk.

As soon as this was done, Jake climbed up into the vault and with his cleverly designed brackets, he positioned the photos in front of the camera lenses. Then, he went back down the ladder and rejoined both feeds. Now if anyone was monitoring the cameras, all they would see was an empty vault. He hoped that the temporary loss of signal would be dismissed as merely a glitch. It occurred to Jake that most of the security precautions were designed to stop anyone getting into the vault, once you were inside, there was little to worry about. There were, of course, the two cameras and there were pressure sensors under the pile of gold bars. If you removed so much as one gold bar, the weight difference would be detected, and the alarm would be activated.

The alarm would sound both inside and outside the bank, but also, it would alert the manager and the local police station. It was fortunate, therefore, that the gold would not be touched.

Once everyone had entered the vault, they went to work. Because gold bars would be very heavy to carry and difficult to change into money, Lee had told them to take out only the bundles of £50 notes, bonds and any jewellery found in the safe deposit boxes. Harry started drilling out the safe deposit box locks, while the others were filling their bags.

Having filled all their bags to capacity, they descended into the storm drain. Because the bags were so heavy, they couldn't manage the equipment at the same time. The answer was to leave the equipment behind and return later.

Lee had told Jake to leave the photos in place, so the subterfuge could be extended. No one would know that the vault had been robbed, until the staff arrived the next morning. Even then nobody would discover the theft, until one of the staff needed to go into the vault.

They carried their bags and rucksacks to where they had left the van. Then they climbed out of the storm drain and, still enjoying the cover of darkness, they threw their bags into the back of the van. Then, Tim guarded the van while the others returned for the equipment. Now they were rich, They could afford to leave the equipment behind, but they were afraid that they might be traced.

When they came back with the equipment, they put it in the back of the van, strapped the ladder to the roof and they all took their seats. Ben then drove them all to their respective homes.

As soon as Lee had heard from Ben that everyone was safely home, he breathed a sigh of relief and he thought 'Yet another project successfully completed.' Obviously, he had not heard the saying that starts 'don't count your chickens'. For his 'chickens' were definitely still to hatch.

Once they were home, Lee's instructions were quite specific. They were to put the bags somewhere safe and then they were to lay low for three months, not touching the bags. Then they were would all meet to share their ill-gotten gains seven ways.

Most of them adhered to the rules, except Ben.

After a month, he could resist no longer, and he took some notes out of one of the bags. Then he went on a spending spree. Unbeknownst to him, the notes had all been marked with a pen that could only be seen under ultraviolet light.

He bought new clothes, and he went to several restaurants and pubs. Everyone had been alerted of the robbery and advised to check all fifty-pound notes.

Of all the people who reported stolen fifty-pound notes, no one could remember who gave it, except one publican. It was Bens local, and the publican remembered wondering where Ben got that sort of money. He knew that Ben would be coming to the pub that night, so he alerted the police and advised them to come in plain clothes.

When Ben arrived, he was arrested by two plain clothed detectives. Under a fairly intense interrogation, Ben finally cracked and gave up the names and addresses of his five accomplices. He was unable to help them with Lee, because he didn't know his last name or address.

The rest of the team were soon rounded up and the loot confiscated.

Meanwhile, back at the lock up, Lee was aware that the three months rental would soon be coming to an end, so he renewed for a further three months.

When the court case finally arrived, most of

them were tried together, but Ben wanted a separate trial. This was because he had been told by the police that in return for his cooperation, he would receive a lighter sentence and he didn't want the others to know. He told the others that he had been tried separately, because he had been arrested first and by a different detective.

It had been well over a month and Lee had not heard from anyone. He decided to phone everyone in the team, but all he was met with was an answering machine. Each time, he left a message, but after two days, he had received no replies.

Lee knew that this could mean only one of two things. Either they had shared the money six ways and cut him out altogether or they had been caught. Lee didn't think it was the first option because at least one or two of them would have told him.

He started to think of all the ways he might be at risk.

Lee had been very careful to with-hold his full name and home address from the team and anything he had purchased was with cash and he always gave a false name and address. Similarly, he had paid the first three months rental in cash.

Lee heard from one of his sources that the whole team had indeed been arrested, so he thought that the only appropriate course of action was to leave the lock up and never return. This was, after all, the only address that was known. He was ok at home for two days, but then he remembered that he had foolishly renewed the lock up rental using his credit card. He was confident that the rental company wouldn't be running any checks, but he was sure that the police would. It was only a matter of time before they knew his full name and address. He packed two suitcases and headed for the airport. He then flew to Spain. He knew that he would miss his beloved England, but he could never return, for fear of being arrested.

As soon as he arrived in Spain, he opened a bank account, and he asked his bank to transfer all his savings. He would have to be content with having pulled off a very daring raid, as he had nothing to show for it. Fortunately, he had substantial savings to fall back on.

He then phoned his estate agent, asking them to sell his house and to put the proceeds in to a Swiss bank account. He said that he would be sending them the keys to the house, and he would be including the Mercedes and all the furniture. He was careful to with-hold his phone number and he mailed the keys from Germany, because he didn't want anyone to know that he was in Spain.

Meanwhile, back in England, five of the team were sentenced to serve ten years behind bars. Ben had helped the police, so he was only sentenced to serve two years.

The banks insurance company had paid to have all the repairs carried out, on the condition that the bank upgraded its security measures inside the vault. The police had returned all the stolen items to the bank. Once the bank had taken everything that belonged to it, some of the safe deposit box holders laid claim to the rest of the bonds. However, no one would own up to knowing anything about the money or the gems. Of course, some of them didn't have either of them in their box, but the others didn't want to answer any awkward questions which might be asked by the police. Consequently, the bank inherited a small fortune.

On the other hand, Ben had helped the police, so he was only sentenced to two years.

A few of the safe deposit box holders took their custom elsewhere, but most of them stayed, secure in the knowledge that the bank would be installing additional security in order to ensure that such an audacious robbery could never be repeated. Afterall, the bank had a certain reputation to maintain. Hence the saying 'As safe as the Bank of England. '

Acting on information received, the police raided the lock up, but they found no one there.

Furthermore, they found nothing to give them the full name or address of Lee.

Meanwhile, a very irate homeowner had phoned the police to report an abandoned vehicle that was outside their house. She explained that it had been there for over a month. She had tried phoning the number on the side of the van but all she got was an answer message, which said that they were not taking on any new business. She wondered if they had gone out of business. Two officers attended the scene and saw that the van belonged to a window cleaning company. They tried to phone the number and to their surprised the phone was answered by a Detective Sergeant.

PC Vic Wakeman shared all the information he had on the van, including its description and where and when it had been abandoned.

When the phone call had ended, DS Don Van Leer looked up the location of the van on the map. He discovered that the van had been abandoned just around the corner from where Ben lived. Not only that, but the van had also been abandoned on the day of the robbery. Don drew the instant conclusion that the van must have been the vehicle used to make good the robbers escape.

PC Vic Wakeman phoned a local locksmith who he had used before and asked him to attend immediately. When the locksmith arrived, the officer asked him to open the van and to show him how to hotwire the ignition.

Meanwhile, the sergeant sent a forensics expert to the scene. As soon as he arrived, he dusted the inside of the van for fingerprints.

After he had finished, the two officers drove the van back to the station, as instructed by the sergeant. Once there, the van would be impounded, until the criminals were safely in prison.

The detective's searched for several days looking for an address for Lee. Finally, they had a lucky break and learned from the agent who rented the lock up to Lee, that he had used his credit card to renew the contract. The agent gave them the name of the issuing bank.

One of the detectives phoned the bank and obtained a full name and address for Lee. The sergeant went to the address with one of his detectives.

Once they reached the address, the sergeant produced a set of skeleton keys, which he used to open the front door. The detective was amazed at how skilfully his sergeant used the keys. The sergeant explained that his actions were strictly illegal, and it was better for him to say nothing.

They searched the house from top to bottom but found nobody. Realising that there was little point in prolonging the search, they decided to leave.

As they were leaving, someone was erecting a 'for sale' sign at the front of the house. Having made a note of the name and phone number of the estate agents, they returned to the station.

Once back at the station, one of the detectives phoned the estate agent and was told that Lee was selling the house and was apparently living in Germany. They knew that, as all the stolen items had been returned to the bank and most of the gang had been arrested, there would be no chance of obtaining an extradition of order from Germany. Little did they know that Lee was in Spain. Lee would have to remain the one who got away.

Two years after the gang had been incarcerated, two prison officers came to escort Ben to see the governor of the prison. None of the others knew that he was about to be discharged, so he told his cell mates that he was going to complain about the food. By the time they discovered the truth, he would have been released and, before they were discharged, he would be long gone with his wife and kids.

Meanwhile, in sunny Spain, Lee was relaxing on a lounger, on a beach, somewhere in Malaga. For the last two years, he had worked on his upper body strength and now he was able to transfer himself in and out of his wheelchair without assistance. Also, he was sporting an impressive suntan. Back in England, his house had sold quickly. The buyer was happy to accept all his furniture and the Mercedes was a bonus. The estate agent had transferred the proceeds to Lee's account in Switzerland and Lee had moved it to Spain. Once he had the money, he had bought a house in Malaga.

Lee leant forward, thinking of all the things that he missed about England. Then he finished his cocktail, summoned the waiter to bring him another. Then he lay back on his lounger, enjoying the warmth of the sun on his face and he didn't give England another thought.

The teacher

Although she was christened Elizabeth, for as long as she could remember, everybody had called her Liz.

Two years after she had started at Infant School, she was so besotted with her teacher that she decided she would grow up to be one.

Often, when she was at home, playing with her dolls, she would sit them behind their little desks and arrange them into a classroom. Then she would stand at the front of the class and lecture to them, as if she were already a teacher.

All through Junior School, she hung onto the conviction that one day she would be a teacher. When Liz started at Senior School, she was even more sure of her chosen vocation.

By the third year she had displayed quite an aptitude for languages.

The following year, Liz was expected to pick the O levels she wished to take. She chose ten, including German, French and Italian.

She passed all of them, but her highest grades were in the three languages. Therefore, it was no surprise that she went on to take the three languages at a level.

Liz passed all three of her A levels, with an A grade in French, her best and favourite subject.

Armed with these qualifications, she started applying to several of the teacher training colleges. She was offered a placement at all of them, so she chose the college which was nearest to where she lived.

Once Liz had graduated, she was finally able to teach, something which she had longed for since she was six.

She started teaching first and second year kids, at a local high school and soon she became very popular. By the second year, Liz had become a firm favourite with most of the kids.

Only two years later, she found herself teaching fourteen- to sixteen-year-olds. Her aim was to coach them through o level French.

Most of her pupils were very well behaved and took their studies very seriously. However, one fourteen-and-a-half-year-old boy named Alfie Byrd was often late for class. Unfortunately, his French lesson was the first one of the day, so if he was late for school, he was also late for his French lesson. When he did arrive, he was most disruptive, so he was often given detention.

One day, after school, Liz found him dealing drugs, outside the school gates. She gave him a dressing down, but she said that as it was his first offense, she would be giving him detention and the matter would go no further. However, if she ever caught him dealing drugs again, she would have to inform the headmaster and the police. She explained that she wouldn't be giving him detention that day, as she had personal matters to attend to, but he would have detention the following day.

The next day, after school, Liz or Miss Jones, as she preferred to be addressed by her pupils, waited in anticipation of Alfie's arrival. However, he never arrived. She waited for another hour, but he still didn't come. She was left with no other choice but to inform the headmaster and the police.

The following morning, she did just that and, as it was a Friday, she didn't hear until the Monday morning that Alfie had left the school, never to return. He was still pedalling drugs, but he was doing so in a different place.

Liz quickly informed the police of this and very soon after, they arrested Alfie and later charged him with selling class A drugs.

Liz heard of his arrest and when the date of the

court case had been set, she resolved to attend.

On the day of the court case, Liz arranged for one of her colleagues to cover her lessons. She learnt from the various testimonies that Alfie was from a broken home. A year before, his father had left, and his mother was an alcoholic. Being the eldest of seven children, it fell to him to look after them all. He was found guilty as charged, but when it came to sentencing, the judge was very lenient. Considering Alfie's age, the fact that it was his first offense and he his circumstances, he was only ordered to serve six months in a juvenile correction facility.

When Alfie was released, he was well over fifteen. He went straight to his old school to apologise to Miss Jones and to ask her if he could help in any way. She agreed to take him on as her classroom assistant. As he wouldn't be paid until he was sixteen, she paid him out of her own pocket.

As Alfie's sixteenth birthday approached, Miss Jones was really feeling the financial strain of subsidising him. She had used half her savings, so she decided to ask the headmaster if he would start paying Alfie, as soon as he reached 16. He agreed to put Alfie on the payroll, but at a reduced rate.

Things continued very well, until some of the female teachers started noticing money missing from their handbags. Most of them couldn't tell exactly how much had been taken, but one lady had just been to the bank, so she was sure that a £10 note was missing.

A few days later, Miss Jones caught Alfie rifling through a handbag that had been left hanging on the back of a chair. She told him that this would have to stop.

He explained that he just couldn't live on the money which he received. Miss Jones agreed to continue subsiding him as long as he stopped stealing.

Alfie decided that he couldn't allow her to keep giving him money, because she had always been so kind to him. Therefore, he chose instead to leave the school.

The following day, Alfie resumed his drug dealing. He knew it was wrong, but it was a very easy way to make money.

He was doing very well but unfortunately; his good fortune was short lived. He was arrested by the police, who were keeping a close eye on him.

This time the judge was not so lenient on him, because of his age and it being a repeat offence. Alfie was found guilty of selling class A drugs, and he was sentenced to spend two years in prison.

It was perhaps inevitable that as soon as Alfie found himself a in prison, he was adversely influenced by some of the inmates. After all, he was at a very impressionable age and some of the inmates were hardened criminals. Long before Alfie was released, he was already planning his next crime. It was easy money, as long as you didn't get caught.

As soon as Liz heard that Alfie was in prison, she went to visit him. She was shocked to find that in a short amount of time he seemed to have changed completely. He was now very hard, and his soft side appeared to have vanished.

Liz returned to the school, all the time blaming herself for Alfie's' current situation.

When she arrived at the school, one of her colleagues reassured her, by saying 'You did all you could for the boy, but sometimes, whatever you do, some people can never be helped.'

Liz continued to visit Alfie and eventually, she persuaded him to return to the school, when he was released. By then he would be eighteen, so he would be paid a full wage. It may not be as much as he could get from his criminal activities, but at least it would be honest.

Silence in court

Even as a child, Don showed signs of brilliance and by the time he was fourteen, he displayed a keen interest in the law.

He passed all of his exams and started to apply to a few Universities, in order to read law. Finally, he went to Bath University, which was his favourite. Once he had graduated, he signed up for the Bar exam. Once he had passed, he became a solicitor.

Don worked as a solicitor for many years, handling a multitude of different cases. After this, he found that it wasn't enough, so he sat the exam to become a Barrister.

As a Barrister, he acted as both prosecutor and defence, with cases ranging from divorce and petty theft to rape and murder. Over the years, he earnt himself the reputation of rarely losing a case. He had the power of being a great orator and he was very persuasive with his arguments. This, together with his vast knowledge of the law, enabled him to build a very strong case. Eventually, even being a barrister wasn't enough for Don, so he applied to become a judge.

Don was well aware that to become a judge he would have to accept a considerable drop in income in comparison with the amount that he could earn as a Barrister. However, the job would come with a great deal of kudos.

Don started as a judge at a small, provincial crown court and he slowly worked his way upwards, until he found himself working in London.

Don had a real passion for the law, so for at least two hours a day he would pore over one of his veritable library of law books. He would always buy the latest law books, so he could keep abreast of all the most recent laws passed and the most recent precedents established.

He worked in London for several years, completely unaware that the lord chief justice was keeping a watchful eye on his progress.

The thing he liked most about being a judge was that he didn't have to take sides, but he could always remain impartial.

Out of the blue, Don received a phone call from the clerk to the Lord Chief Justice. He was trying to set up a meeting between Don and the Lord chief.

As the day of the meeting approached, Don feared the worst, but to his great surprise he was invited by the Lord Chief to join the Royal Courts of Justice, otherwise known as the Supreme Court. This was indeed an honour, so he accepted, without hesitation.

Don started as a Mr Justice, with his eyes firmly set on ultimately becoming a Lord Justice.

He tried many cases, some of which required a jury. In these cases, the jury would decide whether or not the defendant was guilty, and it was up to him to pass sentence.

He tried many cases and after several years, he was finally invited to become a Lord Justice.

As a lord Justice, he wore a red silk gown and all the corridors which linked his chambers to the courts were adorned with red carpets. Etiquette would dictate that if you were walking down the corridor and you met a lord Justice coming the other way, you had to step out of the way and let him pass. However, Don didn't agree with such pomp and ceremony, so if he met someone coming the other way, he was just as likely to step out of the way and let the other person by.

Also, as a Lord Justice he was responsible for trying some highly complex cases, some involving high profile celebrities. He preferred it if he didn't know any of the defendants, because it helped him to remain impartial.

He tried many cases in his long and successful career, but the hardest one of all involved an embezzlement. The verdict was inevitable, because the man was caught red-handed, and he pleaded guilty as charged. However, when it came to sentencing, Don had a real problem.

Precedent would dictate that he should receive a custodial sentence. However, the man's wife had died the previous year and he had four children, who would end up in care.

He called for a temporary pause in proceedings, to give himself half an hour to consider the matter, in his chambers.

When he returned, he decided to give the man a suspended sentence of two years. This would allow him to look after his own children, as he wouldn't be spending any time in prison. However, he gave the stern warning that if he were to commit another offence, he would be sent to prison for a long time and he would lose his children.

A short time later, he was summoned by the Lord Chief. Don expected to be reprimanded, for ignoring legal precedent, but instead he was praised, for showing compassion.

Don soon became known as the judge whose extensive knowledge of the law was matched only by his ability to show compassion.

Occasionally, Don was asked to preside over a murder trial at the old Bailey. This always left him with mixed feelings. On the one hand, it came as a refreshing change to work at a different venue. On the other hand, sometimes the case involved some quite unsavoury details.

Don continued to hear many varied cases over several years. Then after a long and successful career he retired, at the ripe old age of eighty, having outlasted two lord chief justices. It might seem very old to be retiring, but there is no prescribed age for a judge to retire. Also, he loved being a judge and he couldn't imagine any other sort of life.

He only retired when he did, because he didn't feel as mentally agile as he once was, and he was slowly losing his memory. Therefore, he retired before he made a serious mistake.

It took him a few months to adjust to the relatively sedentary life of retirement, but once he had, he rather enjoyed it.

Apart from giving him the time to do the many things that he had neglected, he was able to devote more time to his darling wife and his great grandchildren.

He also took up many hobbies and spent the rest of his years, living the quiet life.

Brush strokes

By the time she had started her second year at high school, Hayley was already exhibiting a distinct leaning towards the Arts. Many people, including her parents, had told her that art would never be anything, but a glorified hobby and the real money was to be made from studying maths or science. However, Hayley had already shown her preference and would not be swayed from that decision. Anyway, she had a certain talent for art and didn't like maths or science at all.

Hayley spent some of her third year, discovering the entrance requirements for Art College and as soon as she met those requirements, she started to apply.

When she started at Art College, she was not sure which particular discipline to follow. Therefore, Hayley decided to try all the types of art which they offered, in order to find out which one suited her best.

During the first few months, she tried sketching using charcoal, painting using water colours and oil paints. She also tried sculpturing, pottery and even photography. Finally, she decided that she most enjoyed painting with oils.

By the time Hayley graduated from Art College, she was quite proficient at painting, so she decided to rent a small studio with a flat above. For the first few months, Hayley honed her skill as a painter.

When Hayley thought that her work was good enough, she sold one of her paintings to an acquaintance. Her enthusiasm had been beginning to wane, but her first sale renewed her confidence.

She continued to improve every week and finally she hung all her paintings on the wall and opened her studio to the public.

The first day went very well, but most people came only to view and not to buy. Slowly, her sales increased and so did the prices that she could ask.

As the time rolled on, her standard continued to soar and so did her reputation. Her paintings were now selling for some quite high prices.

After a particularly busy day, Hayley sat, calculating the total of the day's takings. Nearly all the buyers had paid by cheque, but one man had paid in cash. He had also bought the most expensive painting in the collection.

The following day, Hayley took the cheques and

the cash to the bank and to her utter amazement, the bank told her that all the notes were counterfeit. She rushed back to the studio, only to find that the man had not left an address. She could only surmise that in her excitement at having sold her prized artwork, she had neglected to carry out her usual checks. Even if he had given an address, it would almost certainly have been fictitious. As it was, she could be absolutely sure that she had been the victim of a scam. In the circumstances, she had no choice but to accept that she had been swindled out of a lot of money.

Business continued to do very well, until disaster struck. One day, in the middle of the night, a spontaneous fire broke out in the studio, owing to faulty wiring. The whole place should have been rewired years before, but the landlord had failed to do so.

She was woken up by the smoke coming from the studio. She rushed down the stairs, only to find that the studio was a blaze. It was already too late to save any of her paintings, so she went back upstairs to phone for the fire brigade.

The fire brigade came very quickly, but alas were only in time to save the building, not Hayley's paintings.

The following day, the landlord came with some mixed news. His building insurance would pay to rectify the fire damage to the building. However, he confessed that he had no contents insurance, so the painting would not be covered.

Hayley decided to sue him for the loss of her paintings. Unfortunately, the only barrister who she could afford was a junior, so at the court case, he was completely outclassed by the landlord's barrister. Consequently, Hayley not only received nothing to compensate her for the loss of her paintings, but the landlord then sued her for costs.

Hayley was devastated. She not only had nothing left to sell, but all she could look forward to was an enormous legal bill.

Then something happened, which was quite unexpected. When news got out that all her paintings had been destroyed in a fire, her work already out there in the field rose in price exponentially. Some of her paintings started to change hands for huge amounts.

Hayley was just on the brink of giving up entirely, but this turn of events gave her new hope. She found a new, slightly larger premises to rent, with a different landlord.

She told the current landlord that she was aware that normally she should give notice, prior to her departure but in the circumstances, it might be better for both parties for her to leave as soon as possible. Besides, the ground floor was totally uninhabitable.

Hayley loved the new premises, but this time, before she signed any tenancy agreement, she had the presence of mind to ask the new landlord when the place had last been rewired. He answered that the whole place had been rewired only two years ago and he showed her a safety certificate to prove it.

Completely satisfied with his reply, she moved in, without delay. As soon as she was settled, she began to paint again. In doing so, she hoped to test the buoyancy of the market.

The market turned out to be a lot more buoyant than she thought. Her painting was snapped up almost before the paint had dried. Hayley continued to paint during every waking hour, but she still couldn't keep pace with demand. In fact, she used the flat only for eating and sleeping.

Hayley realised that the only way she could slow down demand, was to increase the prices once more. She was reluctant to do this as she already considered the prices to be much too high. However, it seemed to have the desired effect, because demand slowed right down, but was still there. At last Hayley was able to have some leisure time. She would relax in front of the tv. The trouble was that she was asleep before the programme had ended.

After two years, Hayley had become very rich, so she decided to go on a spending spree. First, she bought herself a completely new wardrobe. Then she put down a substantial deposit on a new premises. She also bought a flat in the same row as the other premises. This would mean that she would have to walk to work, but she was sure that she could just about manage the 30 yards or so.

Also, she part-exchanged her little car for a much larger one and she hired Jack to be her driver and odd-job man. She then hired Mary to be her housekeeper. A few weeks later, she discovered that Jack was a keen gardener, so she increased his salary and asked him to sort out her garden, which looked a mess.

Jack had nearly finished the odd jobs and he rarely had to drive, so he spent most of his time in the garden.

Within a few months, the garden was completely transformed, and Hayley thought it looked magnificent.

Mary also received an increase to her salary, and she was asked to make a few meals for Hayley.

Mary started by cooking Hayley one meal a day, but soon she was making her 3 meals a day.

Hayley gave Mary a very generous budget, so she could buy only the finest food. Hayley also told her to buy enough food for herself and Jack.

Hayley had the ground floor restructured, to provide a large studio with an adjacent gallery. She had the upper floor restructured, to provide an office, a storeroom, a lavatory and a kitchen-diner. There was no need for a lounge, because all her relaxing would be done in the flat.

Ten years later, Hayley had become very rich indeed. She had already paid off both mortgages, so she decided to sell the flat and buy a detached house for cash. The house was not far from the studio, but it required a short drive.

As soon as Hayley had bought the studio, she continued to be quite a prolific artist, but now she made sure that she hung one of her paintings in the gallery to replace each one that was sold. Once the gallery was almost full, she employed Cliff to manage it and she opened the gallery to the public.

Cliff was responsible for arranging the times for each tour and how many people could come. He was obviously a born showman, because he loved to show off his extensive knowledge of art in general and more specifically details of each painting.

Most of the people who attended the tour, came only to view and appreciate the work, but occasionally one of the major art dealers would buy a painting for an anonymous client.

When the gallery was full, Hayley started to

stockpile and every time someone bought a painting, it was quickly replaced from stock.

When Hayley reached the age of seventy, she closed the gallery, but she continued to stockpile her paintings.

Hayley was still painting at seventy-eight, but her eyesight was beginning to deteriorate. Consequently, she decided that this was a good time to retire. She continued to paint for herself, because she loved it so much. She knew that none of these paintings would ever be valuable, but it didn't seem to matter.

News of Hayley's retirement soon reached the ears of some of the most eminent art dealers in the world. They all made the same incorrect assumption that there would never be any more of Hayley's paintings going onto the market and they spread the word accordingly. Consequently, her paintings were considered as rare, so their value went up considerably. Hayley already thought that her paintings were valued much too high, but now their value was even higher.

Little did they know that Hayley had a gallery full of paintings, as well as a substantial stockpile.

She was careful to only sell one painting periodically, in order to maintain prices and she sold each piece through an agent; this enabled her to protect her anonymity. This raised enough money for Hayley to continue to live in the manner to which she had become accustomed. She continued to eat fine food and drink fine wine and she took two luxury holidays a year.

Her only regret was that she had never been married. However, her three siblings had all married, long since and had given her five adorable nieces and nephews. They were grown up now, but they still visited their favourite auntie, as often as they could. They would regale her with their latest news, and she would entertain them with her stories, some of which were true. She subscribed to the saying that 'you should never let the truth get in the way of a good story.'

At the age of eighty-nine, Hayley passed away peacefully, in her sleep. She had done very well for most of her working life, but now she became famous. As with most great artists, Hayley was not fully appreciated until after her demise.

A few months later, her paintings were priceless. This was good news for her five nephews and nieces, to whom she had left her entire estate, including a gallery full of paintings.

By selling only one picture every few months, it released enough money to allow them all to leave their jobs and to pursue various types of voluntary work. One became an amateur art critic, one looked after disabled children and one looked after sick animals. Whatever they did, they were kept happy for the rest of their lives. None of them ever forgot that this was all thanks to auntie Hayley.

The lasting friendship

Sean and Leo had met when they were both only four years of age and they soon became very firm friends-this was a friendship that would endure throughout their lives. This was largely because they had similar views on most subjects.

One subject on which they were violently opposed was religion. You see, Sean was a staunch Roman Catholic and Leo was a life-long atheist.

When they were in their late teens, they had a very heated argument about religion. The argument almost resulted in blows, when Leo diffused the situation, by declaring religion to be a taboo subject, never to be discussed again. They both agreed to disagree, and they got on with their lives.

The only other subject on which they differed was that of the spirit world. Leo was a great believer in ghosts, and he claimed to have seen one. Sean, on the other hand, thought that it was nothing but mindless superstition.

After a particularly extended row about spirits, Sean went to bed, still thinking 'what a ridiculous thing to believe in.'

It took Sean a long time to fall asleep and before he did, the temperature in the room fell considerably. He then felt an icy touch on his face and something ruffled his hair. Despite this, he could see nothing.

In the morning, Sean dismissed the whole experience as a bad dream.

That night, the same thing happened. Before Sean fell asleep the air temperature fell suddenly and he feared the worse. The wardrobe door opened and some of his clothes came flying out and landed on his bed. Then a shoe came flying through the air and thumped against the wall, before falling to the floor. Finally, the door opened, then closed again and the room temperature returned to normal.

On the third night, Sean sat up in bed, fearing that the ghost would return, but it didn't.

The following day, Sean met up with Leo and told him what had happened. Then reluctantly Sean confessed that he had changed his mind about ghosts.

This gave them another subject to discuss, without losing their temper.

All was going well between them for the next

few months, until Sean's girlfriend, Jill, decided to seduce Leo. Leo knew that for the sake of his friendship with Sean, he should resist, but he found her very attractive, so he succumbed and slept with her.

In the morning, Leo was riddled with guilt and, although she obviously regarded it as a one-night stand, he decided to own up to Sean.

Sean was furious and told Leo that he never wanted to see him again.

Months later, Sean discovered that, although It was only a one-night stand with Leo, she had been unfaithful to him on several occasions before and since.

Once Sean discovered the full extent of Jill's infidelity, he confronted her with the sordid facts.

Inevitably, there then ensued a huge and violent row, during which they hurled home truths, or at least half truths, at one another.

Finally, the argument culminated in Sean telling his girlfriend that their relationship was at an end.

It took a while for Sean to come to terms with this change in his life, but when he did, he went straight away to find Leo.

When he caught up with Leo, he explained that he and Jill were no longer an item. He also said that from what he had learnt about Jill he was almost certain that she had instigated Leo's one nightstand. Besides this, Sean didn't want a thing like this to come between them, after a life-long friendship.

Once all had been forgiven, the friends embraced and promised that they would never again let anything come between them. They were once more friends and they hoped that it would be a friendship that would last a very long time.

They had their fair share of arguments, but none of them were very serious and they always managed to resolve their differences before the sun went down. It was a friendship that would endure throughout their lives.

Santa, where are you?

Poor little Jimmy was only five years of age when he lost his daddy to cancer. Jimmy loved his daddy, so he never wanted to lose him, especially not at the age of twenty-nine. His Daddy had been struggling with cancer for some time, but he had finally lost the fight.

By the time jimmy was seven, he had reached the conclusion that his daddy must have had a special relationship with Santa. While his daddy was alive, Santa nearly always brought what Jimmy had asked for in his letter. For the last two Christmas's, it was as if Santa had not even read his letter. Last Christmas Jimmy had asked for a bicycle, but all he had received was a bar of chocolate. It was a big bar of chocolate and tasted very nice, but it was hardly a substitute for a bike.

The truth was that Liv, his mummy, was struggling to live on a single income. By the time she had paid all the bills, there was just enough left of her meagre salary to put food on the table. When it came to Christmas, she had no money left.

A year later, she received a long-awaited promotion. This helped to ease her financial situation considerably. Now they could afford to eat much better and she could afford to buy jimmy a much better Christmas present. She still couldn't run to anything as extravagant as a bicycle, but she bought him the best present that she could afford.

Jimmy had just passed his 10th birthday and he had stopped believing in Santa, when against all expectations his mum won a tidy sum of money on the lottery. It was only one month before Christmas, so she bought Jimmy a bicycle.

After some research, Liv discovered that the most popular bike for Jimmy's age group was the chopper, so she bought him a top-of-the-range one.

On Christmas morning, the look of delight on Jimmy's face, when he saw the bike by the tree, was priceless. It was too difficult to wrap, so it just bore a gift tag which read 'To Jimmy sorry that it has taken so long love Mum.'

Jimmy loved the bike and rode it everywhere he went. The first time he rode it to school, he was the envy of all his friends.

Jimmy was very proud of his bike and rode it every day. However, after two years, he rode it to school and left it unattended and unlocked. Inevitably, it was stolen.

Jimmy was devastated and he didn't know how to tell his mum. To his surprise, Liv took it very well and said that she would buy him a new bike, but this time he had to promise to always keep it locked.

As Jimmy was now twelve, she asked him if he might like a bigger bike, as he had grown out of his chopper. Jimmy agreed, so his mum bought him a bike with twenty-six-inch wheels, along with a sturdy lock.

This time, Jimmy promised to take better care of it. Again, Jimmy enjoyed riding the bike every day, Including riding to school.

One fine summers day, Jimmy was cycling along a quiet country road, without a care in the world. He was just enjoying the warmth of the sun on his face when a car came speeding past, much too close for comfort. A short time later, another car sped past him, but this time it was even closer. The nearside door mirror clipped his handlebar, sending his bike into an uncontrollable wobble and throwing Jimmy onto the grass verge. Apparently, the driver hadn't even noticed the incident because he didn't even slow down, let alone stop. Fortunately, the bike only sustained a few scratches on the frame, and jimmy suffered only a few scrapes on his knees and elbows. His hands were protected by his gloves which were ruined in the process. His helmet almost certainly saved his life as he head butted a tree

Jimmy took a few minutes to compose himself, and then, he reluctantly got back on the bike and continued along the road. He left the road at the first opportunity and did not use the roads again for quite some time.

When Jimmy felt confident enough to get back on the road, he used them as little as possible and always during the hours of daylight.

He was able to ride to school without using roads and during the winter, he always used lights.

As Jimmy approached his fifteenth birthday, he had grown exponentially, so his Mum decide to buy him his first adult sized bike. On his birthday, she surprised him by taking to the local cycle shop. Once they were there, she had him measured for the frame size. She then ordered a custom-made bike with an ultra-light weight carbon-fibre frame and twenty-seven- inch carbon-fibre wheels. She then asked for the best gears and brakes available, and Jimmy chose the handlebars, saddle and pedals.

Time seemed to pass very slowly indeed as Jimmy awaited the arrival of his first ever custom-made bike. It was delivered approximately one month after it was ordered, although to Jimmy it seemed much longer.

Jimmy was amazed to find how light it was. He was able to pick it up with one finger. Despite its light weight it was stronger than all traditional bikes with steel or aluminium frames.

The bike was a joy to ride, and Jimmy had chosen drop handlebars for two reasons. They were more conducive to the racing position and were much less likely to be knocked by a passing car.

Although Jimmy's accident was a long time ago, it still haunted him to this day.

Whenever Jimmy left the bike unattended, he was careful to use his new lock. This lock incorporated a long chain which enabled him to secure both wheels and the frame. The chain could, of course, be cut with bolt cutters, but any opportunist was unlikely to be carrying a pair. The bike was very desirable, so in order to dissuade any professional thief, he always left the bike in busy areas, with plenty of passers-by. This would make it extremely difficult for anyone to use bolt cutters without being seen.

Soon after the bike was delivered, it was Christmas, so Liv bought him all the Lycra gear together with some special cycling gloves and shoes. Finally, she bought him a state-of-the-art helmet, to give him maximum protection.

For several weeks prior to his seventeenth birthday, all Jimmy could talk about was that soon he could drive a car. With this in mind, his mum bought him a brand-new car for his birthday. For this she used most of her substantial winnings and, as an early Christmas present, she also paid for the first year's road tax and insurance.

Each model of Jimmy's car came with electric windows, central locking, immobiliser and alarm included, but his particular model offered a sporty engine, an aerofoil (otherwise known as a wing), at the back and extra-large diameter alloy wheels. The wheels were also extra wide and came with low profile tyres. These were excellent for cornering but were horrendously expensive to replace. At low speed the wing was merely for show as it did very little, but once out on the open road, it really came into its own. At high speed it exerted down-force on the back of the car, giving the wheels better traction. The car boasted a fairly powerful engine and was rear wheel driven, so good traction became all important.

By the time the car had arrived, Jimmy had been working for several weeks, so he was able to pay for driving lessons. He also started saving for servicing and maintenance.

Some of Jimmy's friends were older than him and had already passed their driving test. They were happy to act as supervisor while Jimmy was driving on L plates.

Jimmy was never short of offers during the evening, so he could drive them to pubs and night clubs. He would be the permanently designated driver while they could all drink

After a few weeks, Jimmy started to feel used. He would drive four of his friends to and from the pub. On the way there, one of them would act as his supervisor. But on the way back, they would all be drunk and half asleep, so none of them would be any use to him at all. While he was still a learner, he went along with the charade, but as soon as he passed his driving test, things would have to change radically. He would still be prepared to be the nominated driver occasionally, as long as his friends reciprocated.

Once he had passed his test, Jimmy drove his car almost every day. Sometimes he drove a distance that only a car could achieve.

Of course, Jimmy never forgot his bike, which he rode at least three times a week. This helped him maintain his level of fitness, it kept him close to nature and it gave him a sense of freedom that only a bike could do.

When the car was new, it cost little to run, because nothing needed to be replaced. However, after a while many things started to wear out, including the tyres and the exhaust.

After three years, the MOT fell due. The first

was relatively cheap, but subsequent MOTs began to cost quite a lot just to keep the car roadworthy. Jimmy was proud to be the owner of a car, but as the bills soared, he became less enchanted.

In a moment of reflection, he thought about a time when he was very small, because life was much less complicated, and he still believed in Santa.

The actor

Ken loved acting, he started at school when he joined the drama class. From the first day he showed a certain amount of talent for it and before long he was playing main parts. He developed an ability to connect with the audience, an ability that would stand him in good stead in the future.

At fifteen years old he joined a theatre centre, and he quickly identified the best actors so he could emulate them. At eighteen years of age, he also joined a local amateur dramatic society, so he was rehearsing most nights. By this time, he was particularly good and nearly always played the lead part. At twenty-one, he decided to become a professional actor, so he applied to RADA, he was still living with his parents, so they agreed to support him for the next three years. RADA accepted him on the basis that he would pay a full fee for the first year. They were so impressed with him in his first year that they granted him a full scholarship for the next two years.

For three years Ken worked extremely hard, and his tutors were pleasantly surprised at his progress. He was good when he arrived at RADA but now, he was superb. Although he had worked very hard, Ken dreaded having to leave because he had enjoyed his time at RADA very much. Also, he knew that he would miss all his tutors and his many friends. However, he was also excited about the prospect of embarking on a career in professional acting. Besides, he was sure that he would be returning to see his tutors and he would keep in touch with some of his friends.

He knew that when he started acting, he would be unknown so he would only get small parts but all the directors with whom he worked were very impressed with the way he always gave one hundred percent to every role whatever the size of the part. They also noticed how quickly he could establish a rapport with the audience. Consequently after a few months he started to win much bigger parts and within a year he was playing main parts and even the occasional lead.

Even the prompts notice that he learnt his lines so well that he never needed a prompt. The audience also noticed how he could command the stage. He had brought with him from his years as an amateur actor the habit of reading through the scripts before every performance. It may have been only a superstition but if it worked, he was not about to stop.

For years Ken seemed to go from strength-to-strength riding on his reputation as an actor. Then the inevitable happened, he was playing the lead in a particularly wordy play when he dried and completely forgot his next line. Ken stood rooted to the spot staring at the audience for what seemed like an eternity but was in fact less than a minute. It only took the prompt that long because it took him completely by surprise. After all Ken never needed a prompt. Ken was very relieved to finally get the prompt and the scene proceeded to the end without any further problems. It was lucky that it was the last scene of the play. It was even more fortunate that this was the last performance of an exceptionally long run. Ken could not understand how he could have forgotten his line. He had after all done the scene hundreds of times before. He took it so badly that he missed the after-show party and went straight home. He sat in his armchair staring mindlessly at the television while he brooded on his mistakes. The only thing that was different about that day is that he had been so busy that he had not even glanced at his script. For the first few weeks his agent phoned him every day with a new part for him to consider. Each time Ken turned the part down flat without ever seeing the script. Eventually the agent became tired of Kens' negativity, and he stopped phoning. Ken had lost his confidence, so he decided never to return to the stage.

About a week later he received a phone call from his favourite director asking if he could come to see him. Ken was delighted that the director would even think of him. A few days later the director came and after they had exchanged pleasantries, they both sat down. Cutting to the chase the director said that he completely understood what he was going through but if he continued going down this road, he ran the risk of everyone forgetting him. He went on to say that some of the best actors in the world have taken a prompt at least once in their career. The important thing was to accept it and move on. Ken seemed to be taking all this in but as soon as the director had left, he returned to sitting in his armchair staring at the television.

After a week he received an unexpected parcel. It was a script from the same director who had come to see him. The covering note said that he might find this play of interest and he thought that Ken would be very good as the lead. The director also said that if he wanted the part a phone call would secure it for him. Ken reluctantly started to read the script but once he had started, he could not put it down. It was a wonderful play, and the lead part was to die for. He immediately phoned the director to accept the part. Ken was given a date for the first full read through of the script and as the day approached, he felt the nerves building in him to the point at which he was more nervous than he had been for the audition for RADA. As soon as he arrived at the venue for the reading and realised that he knew most of the cast he was much more relaxed. Everyone was pleased to see him and some of the people who he had worked with before said that they were looking forward to working with him again.

The rehearsal went very well, and everyone agreed that it was a particularly good play. When they started to rehearse on the theatre stage, Ken realised that it was a theatre which he had performed in many times before, so he felt at home. The rehearsals continued to go well, and the play was ready long before opening night. This gave them the luxury of having time to perfect their moves and their various nuances. The play opened to rave reviews and the audience loved it almost as much as they loved Ken, one reviewer went as far as to say that Ken was giving the performance of his life. Ken was inclined to agree because he had never been more suited to a part.

The cast all agreed that the play was so good it was destined to run for a very long time. They were right because it ran for ten years. Some of the older members of the cast retired at the end of the run as they could not think of a better way to end their career. It only ended when it did because the director felt it was the right time to finish leaving the audience wanting more. Ken kept up his habit of always reading through the script before every performance and he never needed a prompt.

Epilogue: A note from the author Paul Allen

I would like to end with a true story of two icons of the theatre who agreed to volunteer their services to co-star in a play to raise money for charity. As with many plays which are performed for a charity it was very under-rehearsed. What made matters worse was that it was a new play, so nobody knew the lines.

At one stage the two icons were doing a scene together and in the middle of a very long speech one of them forgot their lines. Being a consummate professional, he went into an adlib which was completely in accordance with the rest of the script. No one in the audience would have even known that this was not part of the play.

When he thought that the time was right the other actor joined in and together, they created what was, in effect, a new sub-plot for the play. The poor boy acting as prompt was only substituting for his friend and had never done the job before. He was at a loss to find where they were in the script. He then eventually realised that the actors were no longer following the script and he had just found the ideal line to get them back on track when they ran out of ideas and stood staring at each other.

The prompt was then placed in a dilemma, how do you prompt two such greats of the stage? He decided to whisper the line, but no one seemed to react. He then said the line in a normal voice but still no one reacted. Thinking that they were both a bit hard of hearing he bellowed the line. Finally, one of the actors said, 'Yes, dear boy we both know the line but which of us has to say it?'

THE END

Acknowledgements

I would like to dedicate this book to my beloved wife, Liz, who has always encouraged me to continue, at times when I wanted to stop. I owe a special thanks to Sarah, who translated and typed most of the stories. I would also like to thank Liz for editing the stories. At this time, I would like to remember those who have departed of this life, during the writing of this book, they include my Aunty Betty, Graham Kembey and David White from my Church, Trevor and Paul from my old Church and my friends Hayley, Cathy and Mike, and Don, my favourite teacher.

The husband of Diane whom I mentioned in my last book, Caleb, a good man who died too young doing God's work in Africa.

As a late addition I would like to remember Brenda Searle. The shocking news of her passing only reached me fairly recently. It was both sudden and completely unexpected. R.I.P. Brenda.

I would like to end by remembering our late Queen Elizabeth II (1926-2022). May God protect her.